THE FOLLY

THE FOLLY

Being the Fourth Volume of
The Daughters of Mannerling

Marion Chesney

Chivers Press • G.K. Hall & Co.
Bath, England   Thorndike, Maine USA

This Large Print edition is published by Chivers Press, England, and by G.K. Hall & Co., USA.

Published in 1998 in the U.K. by arrangement with Lowenstein Associates.

Published in 1998 in the U.S. by arrangement with St. Martin's Press, Inc.

U.K. Hardcover ISBN 0–7540–3125–X (Chivers Large Print)
U.S. Softcover ISBN 0–7838–8288–2 (Nightingale Collection Edition)

The text of this Large Print edition is unabridged.
Other aspects of the book may vary from the original edition.

Set in 16 pt. New Times Roman.

Printed in Great Britain on acid-free paper.

British Library Cataloguing in Publication Data available

Library of Congress Cataloging-in-Publication Data

Chesney, Marion.
    The Folly / Marion Chesney.
        p. (large print) cm.—(Daughters of Mannerling ; 4th v.)
    ISBN 0–7838–8288–2 (large print : sc : alk. paper)
    1. Large type books.   2. Inheritance and succession—England—Fiction.   3. Young women—England—Fiction.   4. England—Social life and customs—19th century—   I. Title.   II. Series: Chesney, Marion. Daughters of Mannerling ; 4th v.
[PR6053.H4535F65   1998]
823'.914—dc21   97–30901

CHAPTER ONE

Yet ah! why should they know their fate,
Since sorrow never comes too late,
And happiness too swiftly flies?
Thought would destroy their paradise.
No more; where ignorance is bliss,
'Tis folly to be wise.

THOMAS GRAY

Rachel walked slowly back to Brookfield House. It was a blustery spring day. Her muslin skirts blew about her body. She had been on a walk to Mannerling, her old family home, and it had distressed her to see it still lie empty and neglected. Her sister Abigail had promised her a Season in London, but Rachel was reluctant to go.

Like her five sisters, she had been obsessed with the idea of somehow regaining Mannerling, but she had persuaded herself that the stupid dream was long gone. It was only natural that she should want to see the great house she had once loved lived in again.

Now three sisters were married and gone, and there was only she herself, Belinda, and Lizzie left. They must, she reflected, be among the most highly educated females in the land, for their mother, Lady Beverley, still retained the services of an excellent governess, Miss Trumble, although the girls had overgrown the services of one. Lady Beverley's real reason was that the governess miraculously knew how to soothe her frequent headaches and did not seem to notice on quarter-day that her mistress had 'forgotten' to pay her.

Rachel entered the back garden of the house by a circuitous route. She did not want anyone to know she had gone out walking without a maid.

She went up to her room and changed out of her walking clothes. Lessons were now reduced to two hours in the afternoon. Lizzie bounced into her room, her red hair flying. 'No lessons,' she crowed. 'We are to make a call.'

'Where?'

'Mary Stoddart—I mean, Mary Judd.'

Rachel's face darkened. The vicar's daughter had married one of the previous owners of Mannerling, a Mr. Judd. Mr. Judd had committed suicide, but during her brief reign as mistress of Mannerling, Mary had triumphed over the Beverley sisters.

'Why should we go there?' demanded Rachel. 'We hardly ever call.'

'She sent a note to say she had momentous news. Mama is indisposed. She says Miss Trumble must go with us instead.'

'What ails Mama now?'

Lizzie gave an unladylike shrug. 'Oh, you know. It is always this and that. In fact, she will probably brood over the accounts books.'

Ever since the late Sir William Beverley had lost Mannerling due to his gambling debts, Lady Beverley had become something of a miser. Her three elder daughters had all married well and often sent money, and it was only due to the frequent goading of Miss Trumble that the purse-strings were loosened. Miss Trumble had a way of pointing out that the Beverleys were not living in a way due to their position, which often spurred Lady Beverley on to buying new dresses for her remaining daughters and coals for the fires.

'Mary is always over-exercised about something trivial,' said Rachel. 'But it will come as a welcome break from the schoolroom. We surely do not need any more schooling. Mama says that gentlemen prefer stupid women.'

'And Miss Trumble,' pointed out Lizzie, 'says that the only gentlemen worth having are the ones that appreciate a woman with a brain.'

'Miss Trumble is unmarried,' countered Rachel. 'When do we leave?'

'In ten minutes. Miss Trumble has been looking for you. Where were you?'

She looked at Rachel's muddy pattens, lying discarded in a corner of the room.

'I went for a walk to Mannerling,' said Rachel defiantly. 'Don't you dare tell Miss Trumble. She'll start fretting that I am still in the grip of the old obsession when I was only prompted by a natural curiosity.'

'Was there any smoke from the chimneys? Any carriages?'

'No, still deserted. And there were weeds growing at the side of the drive. The lodge was deserted. So many lost their employ when the Deverses left.'

'The servants were very cruel to us.' Lizzie tossed her red hair. 'We should not mourn their bad luck.'

'I have often thought the servants had reason to dislike us,' said Rachel. 'Do you think this bonnet will do? Oh, why am I bothering about what to wear on a visit to the vicarage? I mean, we treated them like machines, the servants, that is.'

'They were well-housed and well-fed,' pointed out Lizzie. 'I think they behaved very badly. I must prepare myself or Miss Trumble will come looking for me.'

*   *   *

Barry Wort, the odd man, who acted as general factotum, was driving the small Beverley carriage when they set out with Miss Trumble sitting beside him. It was an open carriage. Behind sat the Beverley sisters, Rachel, fair and blue-eyed, Belinda, dark-haired and beautiful in a placid way, and fiery-haired, green-eyed Lizzie.

What would become of them? wondered

4

Miss Trumble. Rachel, the eldest of the three, had grown even more beautiful since the marriage of her twin, Abigail. Her fair hair was almost silver and her eyes large and blue. Abigail had always been the more spirited of the twins, but since she had left and Rachel was no longer in her shadow, the girl seemed more confident, more animated. But how could any gently born miss succeed in the marriage market with only an insignificant dowry? Lady Beverley constantly refused to discuss Rachel's dowry and whether she had increased it from a few hundred pounds. Her three elder sisters' successful marriages made her feel that the Beverleys' luck in that direction had surely run out.

'Why cannot we have a closed carriage?' complained Belinda, holding on to her hat. 'I swear, with the funds Mama must be getting from our married sisters, we could well afford one.'

'Oh, you know Mama,' sighed Rachel. 'But it *is* a bore, for it means on wet days we cannot use the carriage to go anywhere. I wonder what Mary has to tell us.'

'Perhaps she has somehow gained the acquaintance of the mysterious Duke of Severnshire,' said Lizzie.

'I doubt it.' Belinda clutched at her bonnet again. 'The duke is reported to be travelling abroad and is considered to be a bit of a recluse. No one has seen him. When Papa was

5

alive, he and Mama—at Mama's instigation, of course—pretended a strap on the carriage had broken, although Mama got the coachman to cut it conveniently outside the gates of his palace.'

'Oh, I remember,' laughed Rachel. 'Mama was monstrously offended. The duke's servants repaired the strap, the housekeeper served them tea. They were informed his grace was not at home, and yet Mama swears that when they left she saw him looking out of the window.'

'If he is such a recluse, how is it that Mama knew what he looked like?' asked Lizzie.

'Because there was a rather bad portrait of him on display at the town hall at the time.'

'Did she say whether he was handsome?'

'He was accounted very handsome before the visit and nothing out of the common way after it.' Rachel pulled a shawl closer about her shoulders. 'We are nearly there. Miss Trumble,' she called to the erect figure on the box, 'we need not stay long, need we?'

'Not very long,' Miss Trumble called back. 'The sky is getting dark and I fear it might rain.'

'I hope the vicar is not there,' muttered Lizzie. 'He was detestable when he used to oil around us at Mannerling and he is now equally detestable when he patronizes us.'

*   *   *

6

But only Mary was there to greet them, Mary dressed in black and with her black eyes shining with excitement. Mary still wore mourning, not out of grief, but because a tipsy gentleman at an assembly had happened to remark that she looked well in black.

After the ladies were settled in the vicarage parlour, Mary said, 'What news!'

'Well, *what* news?' demanded Rachel crossly.

'Why, Mannerling has been bought.'

'Bought,' chorused the three sisters, their eyes shining while Miss Trumble looked at them with something like dismay on her lined face. 'Who has bought Mannerling?'

'Do let us have some tea,' said Mary, ringing the bell. The sisters waited impatiently while she gave orders to the servant.

'The new owner,' said Mary, 'is a general, retired, of course, General Sir Arthur Blackwood.'

'Retired,' echoed Lizzie in dismay. 'Then he is old?'

'Very old, I believe, and widowed.'

'Might do for Miss Trumble,' muttered Lizzie and then was quelled by a look from that lady.

'But he has a son,' said Mary. 'A widower.'

Their eyes brightened but Mary, infuriatingly—and, Miss Trumble shrewdly thought, deliberately—chose that moment to serve tea and cakes.

'So?' demanded Rachel at last after they had all been pressed to choose and praise seed-cake.

Mary's black eyebrows went up in query. 'The widower,' prompted Belinda.

'He is Charles Blackwood. His wife has been dead these past two years, leaving him with two children, a boy aged eight years and a little girl of six. Mr. Blackwood, the son, was a major in the Hussars, but sold out on the death of his wife. He is accounted very rich.'

'How do you know all this?' asked Miss Trumble curiously.

'His agent was residing at the Green Man at Hedgefield and was engaging servants. They are to take up residence next month.'

'Did you find out how old Mr. Blackwood is?' asked Belinda.

'I believe him to be middle-aged, nearly forty.'

Three faces fell. A widower of nearly forty with two small children did not seem in the least a marriageable prospect.

Mary saw she had lost their interest and said, 'Mr. Blackwood has been seen in Hedgefield and is accounted very handsome.'

But 'nearly forty' had sounded the death-knell of their hopes, for although none of them would admit it, each sister privately held on to that old dream of marrying some owner of their old home and so getting it back.

A few fat drops of rain struck the windowpanes. 'We really must leave.' Miss Trumble got to her feet.

'Such a pity you only have an open carriage,' mourned Mary.

'Just like you, Mary,' said Rachel, adjusting her shawl about her shoulders.

When they had climbed into the carriage, Barry produced umbrellas but the wind had risen, driving the rain into their faces.

Rachel felt very low. It was silly to hang on to the dream of Mannerling, she knew that. But logic warred with emotion in her brain. Nearly forty! A great age. She should write to Abigail and accept the offer of a Season in London. Among the whirl of balls and parties, she would forget Mannerling.

*　　　*　　　*

The days grew milder and the first leaves began to grow on the trees, and still Rachel had made no move to go to London. News of the new occupants of Mannerling began to filter to Brookfield House. The gardens were quickly being restored to their former glory and the temple which Mr. Judd had blown up out of spite and then repaired had been taken down and a new Greek temple, a folly, had taken its place. Rachel felt obscurely insulted by this. Everything should be left as it was. Somehow it was the thought of this folly which drove her into going back to Mannerling, just for one

9

look, just to see if it looked like the old one and whether things were about the same as she so fondly remembered them to be.

One sunny day when Miss Trumble had gone into Hedgefield with Barry and her sisters were playing battledore and shuttlecock in the garden, Rachel slipped out the back way and then set out for Mannerling.

Fluffy clouds sailed across the sky. As she walked along, Rachel wondered for the first time why Miss Trumble had not encouraged her to go to London. Miss Trumble, who would normally have done anything in her power to remove at least one of them from what she called the house's malign influence, was strangely silent on the subject.

As she walked along under the tall trees which arched over the road, with light-green leaves fluttering in the wind, she decided that one last look at Mannerling would be enough. Then she would go back home and send an express to her twin. Only look how deliriously happy Abigail was in marriage, she thought. Perhaps in London there would be a young man waiting for her, someone to love. Her eyes filled with dreams. People called them the unlucky Beverleys, and yet Isabella, the eldest, then Jessica, and finally Abigail had all made successful marriages. 'To men much older than they,' said a little voice in her head.

But Rachel was nineteen and had no intention, or so she told herself, of marrying someone old enough to be her father.

She retreated back into a dream about that young man who was waiting for her in London and was surprised to come out of it in front of the gates to Mannerling. There was smoke rising from the lodge-house and she suddenly did not want to be seen. She walked along the edge of the estate wall to where she knew there was a broken part, but new stone faced her. It had been repaired. She frowned. It had been a convenient way of getting into the estate without being seen. But now she was actually there, it was unthinkable to retreat. She looked up and down the road, but no one was in sight. She grasped the wall firmly and began to climb up. She then balanced on the top, seized hold of a tree branch on the other side and dropped to the ground.

She made her way silently through the trees, nervous now in case a gamekeeper should come across her. She had heard the new folly was on a rise above the ornamental lake.

The Mannerling park was very large, and as she emerged from the shadow of the trees a warm sun struck down on her back and she began to feel tired. But ahead glittered the waters of the lake.

She rounded a stand of alder and there, stretched out in front of her, was the expanse of the lake and on a rise stood the folly. It was a Greek temple made of white marble with slender pillars and a domed top. She had to

11

admit it was even more graceful than the original and was amazed it had been built in such a short time. She looked cautiously about her but there was no one in sight. Rachel walked across the springy turf starred with daisies and entered the temple, which was open all round like a gazebo. There were charming views in every direction.

And then she stiffened, suddenly aware she was not alone. She turned around.

Two children stood there, hand in hand, solemnly surveying her.

The boy had a mop of black curls and large brown eyes. The girl had the same black curls and brown eyes but was younger and smaller. The boy was slim and the little girl still retained a babyish plumpness.

Rachel found she was blushing guiltily. This, then, she thought, must be the Blackwood children.

'Are you from the house?' she asked.

They both nodded.

'Then you must not betray me,' said Rachel. 'I am trespassing. I am Miss Rachel Beverley and I live over at Brookfield House, but Mannerling used to be my family home. What are your names?'

'Beth,' said the little girl shyly, 'and this is my brother, Mark.'

'Are you happy here?' asked Rachel.

She sat down on a stone bench in the middle of the folly and the children sat down on either side of her.

'It is a very grand house,' said Beth tentatively.

'It is the most beautiful house in the world,' said Rachel firmly.

'I don't like it,' said Mark. 'Not at all. It's haunted.'

Rachel gave an indulgent laugh. 'It was never haunted.'

'It is now,' said Mark fiercely. 'By a man who looks like a fox with sandy hair and green eyes.'

Rachel felt a shudder of pure superstitious dread. The boy had described the late Mr. Judd. But then there was a portrait of the late owner, who had committed suicide, hanging in the Long Gallery.

'But you must not tell Miss Terry or she will beat us,' said Mark.

'Is Miss Terry your governess?'

They both nodded.

'And does your father know she beats you?'

Two small heads shook in unison.

'But why not?'

A look of almost adult weariness crossed Mark's face and he gave an unhappy little shrug. 'Father has nothing to do with us.'

Rachel was suddenly sorry for them. 'I used to take a boat out on the lake,' she said. 'Is there still one there?'

Beth's eyes lit up. 'There is a blue one but we are too small to handle the oars.'

'Come along,' said Rachel, standing up. 'I will take you.'

They walked together out of the folly and down the grassy slope to the lake. The small jetty was still there and moored to it was a rowing-boat.

'Are we really going out on the water?' asked Mark, his eyes shining.

'Yes, of course. It's a lovely day and I will make sure you don't fall in.'

She helped them into the little rowing-boat, cautioning them to be careful and sit down gently, and then she took the oars and began to row out into the middle of the lake. The two children sat, enrapt, Mark trailing a hand in the water. The sun was very warm. Rachel shipped the oars, removed her bonnet, and then took up the oars again. She reflected that the children were unnaturally well-behaved for their age.

'I should really take you back,' she said after a while. 'I do not want to be caught trespassing.'

'Oh, just a little longer,' pleaded Mark. 'We are not in the way of having fun, you see.'

Rachel smiled. 'In that case, I will gladly risk disgrace. A little longer.'

The children seemed content to sit there, side by side, facing her as she rowed backwards and forwards across the lake.

And then she saw a look of fear in Mark's face and saw the way he grasped his little sister's hand tightly. 'What is it?' she asked sharply.

'Papa is arrived,' he said in a whisper, 'and Miss Terry.'

Rachel began to row towards the jetty, feeling fury boiling up inside her. The children looked so scared and vulnerable.

As she approached she saw a tall man standing on the jetty, with a thin, bitter-looking woman beside him. Charles Blackwood and Miss Terry.

Charles Blackwood was dressed for riding in a black coat, leather breeches, and top-boots. He had thick black hair, fashionably cut, with silver wings at the side, where his hair had turned white. He had odd slanting eyes of grass-green in a strong, handsome face. He had a tall, powerful figure.

Miss Terry had a crumpled little face, as if years of spite had withered it like a fallen apple. Her eyes were a pale, washed-out blue. Her thin shoulders were bent as though in false humility, but there was nothing humble in her glaring eyes.

Rachel helped the children out onto the jetty and then climbed up after them, aware, despite her temper, of her flushed face and tumbled hair. She realized she had left her hat in the boat.

'You bad, bad children,' exclaimed the governess. 'How dare you escape me! You know what this means?'

They stood before her, heads bowed, hands clasped.

Rachel forgot about Mannerling, forgot about her trespass, and threw back her head, her blue eyes blazing.

'I am Miss Rachel Beverley of Brookfield House,' she said haughtily, 'and yes, the children know what you mean. You will beat them as you have no doubt done many times before.' She rounded on Charles Blackwood. 'Oh, it is not unusual for children to be beaten, but it goes to my heart to see them so white and frightened. Shame on you, sir, for your most abysmal neglect of them. They are charming children and deserve better. They deserve parental love and kindness. Good day to you, sir.'

She marched off, her head high. Temper carried her straight to the drive and down it between the bordering lime-trees, where new leaves as green as Charles Blackwood's eyes fluttered in the wind, to the lodge where the lodge-keeper stared at her in surprise as she opened the little gate at the side of the great gates and stepped out onto the road.

Rachel was too upset to feel dismayed when, as she approached home, she saw her own governess, Miss Trumble, walking to meet her.

'Why, Rachel!' exclaimed the governess. 'What are you doing, walking unescorted and without your hat?'

So Rachel told her about the children and

about what she had said to Charles Blackwood and then waited for a lecture. But, to her surprise, Miss Trumble gave a gentle laugh and said, 'Why, I declare you are become a woman of principle at last. We will say no more about it.'

Rachel decided to write to Abigail and say that she would go to London. The hold Mannerling had held on her had gone. It belonged to a family now, another family, and the fact that it was an unhappy family had nothing to do with her.

*   *   *

But in the morning when she went out to find Barry Wort, the odd man, to give him the letter, she experienced a strange reluctance to hand it over. She tucked it in the pocket of her apron instead. Barry was weeding a vegetable bed, sturdy, dependable ex-soldier Barry, whose common sense had proved of such value in the past.

'Good morning, Barry,' said Rachel. He straightened up and leaned on his hoe and smiled at her.

'We've been getting some uncommon fine weather, Miss Rachel.'

'I went to Mannerling yesterday, Barry,' said Rachel abruptly.

'Well, now, miss, there do be a strange thing. I would have thought you cured of wanting the

17

place.'

'I went for just one last visit.'

'Reckon that place is like gambling, if you'll forgive me for saying so, miss. It's always one last time.'

'I meant it this time. But wait until you hear of my adventure.'

Barry listened carefully to the story of the children and the confrontation. 'You did well,' he said, not betraying that he had already heard the story from Miss Trumble. 'There are beatings and beatings and those motherless children could do with a bit of kindness. What was this Mr. Blackwood like?'

'He is a very fine-looking man,' said Rachel slowly. 'I had heard he was nearly forty and had expected—well, a middle-aged-looking gentleman.'

'Mr. Blackwood already has a good reputation in Hedgefield,' said Barry. 'But any gentleman who settles his bills promptly gets a good reputation. He's caused quite a flurry in the district among the ladies.'

'The widows?'

'No, miss, all the young ladies do be setting their caps at him. He is reputed to be a fine-looking fellow, he has Mannerling and, they do say, a fortune as well.'

The thought flicked briefly through Rachel's mind that she too might set her cap at the master of Mannerling, but then she remembered that grim face and the unhappy children. 'I will not be of their number,' she said lightly. She turned and walked away, and it was only some time later that she realized she still had that letter to Abigail in her pocket.

*   *   *

'You never talk to us any more.' Belinda and Lizzie confronted Rachel later that day. 'Are you going to London? For if you do, you must ask Abigail to invite us as well.'

'I have not made up my mind,' said Rachel loftily. 'And I do talk to you. I am talking to you now.'

'Where were you yesterday morning? You just disappeared and Miss Trumble went out looking for you,' said Lizzie.

'I simply went for a little walk across the fields. Good heavens,' exclaimed Rachel. 'Must I report to you every minute of the day?'

'But what of Mannerling and what of this new owner?'

'You know as much as I do. He is nearly forty, a widower with two children.'

'Do you think he means to entertain?'

'I don't *know*,' snapped Rachel. 'We promised Miss Trumble, if you remember, that we would put all ambitions of regaining Mannerling out of our heads. Why? Would you have me entertain romantic thoughts of a man nearly in his dotage?'

'I suppose it is silly,' said Lizzie. 'But it

19

would be wonderful just to go to Mannerling again.'

Rachel looked at her uneasily. The loss of their home had affected Lizzie more than her sisters, so much so that she had once tried to drown herself. She remembered the little boy, Mark, saying that the house was haunted, and wondered if there was something supernatural about Mannerling that kept them all in its spell.

Betty, the little maid, piped up from the bottom of the stairs, 'A carriage from Mannerling.'

They ran to the window. Their former coachman was driving a carriage. There were two footmen on the backstrap and Rachel recognized in one of them the unlovely features of John, who had once worked for the Beverleys.

'You had best go downstairs,' urged Lizzie, 'for Mama is indisposed.'

'I shall change my gown,' decided Rachel. 'Send Betty to me quickly.'

Miss Trumble received Charles Blackwood in the little parlour, regretting, not for the first time, her mistress's parsimony in leaving the drawing-room unheated.

'I am sorry Lady Beverley is ill,' said Miss Trumble after studying his card. 'I am Miss Trumble, governess to the Beverley sisters.'

His harsh face lightened as he looked down at her from his great height and Miss Trumble wondered rather sadly whether her poor old heart would ever learn to stop beating faster at the sight of an attractive man.

'Then you are the very person I need to see,' he said.

'Indeed? Pray be seated, sir.'

He sat down in an armchair by the fire and looked around him with pleasure. The room was full of feminine clutter—bits of sewing, books, and magazines. There was a large bowl of spring flowers by the window on a round table.

'Were you aware,' began Charles, stretching out his long legs, 'that I met one of your charges yesterday? She left her hat. I brought it back and gave it to the maid.'

'Yes, Rachel. She told me about it. She should not have been trespassing, but she misses her old home.'

'I was grateful to her for bringing to my attention the fact that my children had been subject to harsh attention from their governess. Excuse me, Miss Trumble but there is something faintly familiar about you. Are you sure we have not met before?'

'Oh, no, sir. A governess such as myself, immured in the country as I am, hardly moves in the same circles as such as yourself.'

'Still, there is something . . . Never mind. The reason I am come . . .'

The door opened and Rachel came in, followed by Lizzie and Belinda.

Charles Blackwood got to his feet and bowed. Rachel was very beautiful and seemed even more so than the first time he had seen her, her fair looks contrasting with Belinda's dark-haired beauty and Lizzie's waiflike appeal.

They all sat down.

Charles turned to Rachel. 'I was just beginning to explain to your governess that after your visit yesterday I told Miss Terry, my children's governess, to leave immediately. I am looking for a suitable lady to tutor them and am come to you for help.'

'I think I can help you,' said Miss Trumble, adjusting the folds of a very modish silk gown. Rachel looked at that gown. It was one of Miss Trumble's best, almost as if she had been expecting such a call. 'My girls' schooling has been cut back to a mere two hours in the afternoon, and time lies heavy on my hands. With Lady Beverley's permission, of course, I could offer to tutor your children if they were brought over here every day. My girls could help in their education, and company younger than mine would benefit them.'

'I would be most grateful. Are you sure Lady Beverley will allow you to do this?'

Miss Trumble rose to her feet. 'I will ask her now.'

She left the room with her graceful gliding walk.

'An exceptional lady,' said Charles to Rachel after the door had closed behind the governess. 'Where did your mother come by such a treasure?'

Rachel laughed. 'Our Miss Trumble has certainly made an impression on such a brief acquaintance. What makes you think her a treasure?'

'She has great style and dignity. And I am sure I have met her somewhere before.'

'There is a mystery about Miss Trumble,' said Rachel. 'She appeared one day, without references, references which she swears she will produce if she can ever find them. But she so quickly made herself an indispensable part of the household that none of us can bear to think of her leaving. I trust you will not lure her away from us, sir.'

'Please don't,' put in Lizzie. 'Miss Trumble swore she would stay with us until I am married.'

'And when will that be?' asked Charles. His odd green eyes were full of laughter. Rachel looked at him in surprise. He was certainly changed from the grim-visaged man of the day before.

'I will need to be very lucky,' said Lizzie solemnly. 'You see, none of us has much of a dowry.'

'Lizzie!' hissed Rachel furiously.

'It's true,' said Lizzie defiantly. 'The whole district knows it to be true and Mr. Blackwood will hear it sooner or later.'

'It is not ladylike to discuss money,' pointed

23

out Belinda.

'We talk of nothing else in this house,' muttered Lizzie rebelliously.

Meanwhile Miss Trumble was saying evenly to Lady Beverley, who was reclining on a day-bed in her darkened bedchamber, 'As you say, my lady, I am employed by you. But only see the advantages in my helping Mr. Blackwood with his children. While he is paying me for my services, you need not. Of course, it would probably mean your being invited to Mannerling again and that might distress you. I shall leave you now and tell Mr. Blackwood that I cannot help him—unless I decide to leave you and move to Mannerling. Perhaps that might be a good idea.'

Lady Beverley's face was a study. She was well aware that this elderly and dignified governess not only lent her status but ran her household. She forgot, too, that she had neglected to pay Miss Trumble any salary last quarter-day and said faintly, 'Stay. My poor head. You must realize I am not well and am unable to deal with decisions. But if your heart is set on it, yes, I agree.'

Miss Trumble curtsied and quickly left the room before her employer could change her mind.

When she returned to the parlour, Charles Blackwood looked cheerful and relaxed and Rachel was telling him about an assembly to be held in two weeks' time in the Green Man. 'But perhaps a country hop is too undignified for you, Mr. Blackwood.'

'I have not really engaged in many social entertainments since the death of my poor wife,' he said. 'But yes, I shall probably attend. I hope I can remember how to dance. Ah, Miss Trumble, good news, I hope?'

'Yes, sir. If it is convenient, I think you should bring the children tomorrow morning and we can start as soon as possible.'

He rose to his feet and bowed all around. To his secret amusement, it was Miss Trumble who walked out with him to his carriage, quite like the lady of the house, he thought.

'Perhaps nine o'clock?' said Miss Trumble.

Although she was only a governess, he found to his surprise that he was bowing over her hand.

'Until then.'

John, the footman, let down the carriage steps. Charles climbed inside. John raised the steps and shut the carriage door and turned and gave Miss Trumble a pale, curious, calculating look.

If I gain any influence with Charles Blackwood, thought Miss Trumble, I will tell him to get rid of that gossiping, plotting footman. For she knew that John dreaded any Beverley getting a foothold in Mannerling again because he knew he would lose his job, for he had gone out of his way to be horrible to them.

Inside the house, Rachel was facing her sisters' angry questions. 'You are become secretive, Rachel,' said Belinda. 'Not to tell us you had been to Mannerling and had met the owner. And he is vastly handsome.'

'But a widower with children and much too old,' said Rachel. 'I have no desire to wed a man old enough to be my father.'

Belinda twisted a lock of hair in her fingers and sent Rachel a sideways look. 'I would not find such a man too old,' she said.

Rachel looked at her, startled. Belinda had grown even more beautiful. Her black hair was dressed in one of the fashionable Roman styles which Miss Trumble could create with all the deftness of a top lady's-maid. Her cheeks were smooth and pink and her wide eyes fringed with heavy lashes.

What effect had such beauty on Charles Blackwood? Surely no man could look at Belinda and remain unmoved.

'You are too young, Belinda,' she snapped.

Belinda gave a quiet little smile. 'We'll see.'

'But we promised Miss Trumble that we would put Mannerling from our minds,' protested Rachel. 'Only look at the vulgar reputation we sisters gained in the country by trying to marry previous owners or sons of owners.'

'One son,' corrected Belinda, thinking of the rake, Harry Devers, son of the previous owners, who had caused the Beverleys so much heartbreak. 'Anyway,' she said with a little shrug, 'if Mr. Blackwood has not heard the gossip about us, he soon will, and he will fight shy of us for fear one of the dreadful Beverley girls is going to ensnare him for the sake of his home.'

'Such old gossip,' said Rachel. 'I doubt if he will hear a word!'

CHAPTER TWO

The strongest friendship yields to pride,
Unless the odds be on our side.

JONATHAN SWIFT

Charles Blackwood rode over that afternoon to pay a call on Lady Evans, an elderly widow, accompanied by his father. The old general had known Lady Evans for years and was pleased to learn she resided in the neighbourhood, in Hursley Park.

Lady Evans, a formidable dowager with a crumpled old face under a gigantic, starched cap, welcomed them with enthusiasm. 'General Blackwood,' she hailed Charles's father. 'I declare I have not seen you this age, and you are grown more handsome than ever.'

The general, a genial gentleman with a portly figure and a high colour, bent gallantly

27

over her hand and kissed her fingertips. 'The minute I learned we were to be neighbours, Lady Evans, my poor old heart beat much faster.'

'Silly boy,' she giggled, rapping his shoulder with her fan. 'Now do be seated and I will ring for tea. How do you go on, Charles? So sad about your dear wife. You have two young children, I believe. Well, I hope?'

'I am arranging matters better for them. I have been too distant from my children and it has only just been brought to my attention that their governess was dealing too harshly with them.'

'Children must not be spoilt,' said Lady Evans. The tea-tray was carried in, the spirit stove lit. Lady Evans prepared the tea herself. 'A good beating never harmed a child.'

Charles smiled. 'We must not quarrel on matters of discipline. But they are now in the hands of an estimable governess at Brookfield House.'

'Miss Trumble,' exclaimed Lady Evans. 'She is still there? Why does she not call on me?'

The general looked at her in some surprise. Lady Evans was known to be very high in the instep and it was most unlike her to be pining for a call from a mere governess.

'Miss Trumble was governess to the children of a friend of mine,' said Lady Evans quickly. 'She is out of the common way.'

'I agree,' said Charles.

Her old eyes suddenly narrowed. 'But why does she not reside at Mannerling? Why Brookfield House with those Beverleys?'

'Miss Trumble did not seem anxious to move, so the children are to be taken there every day. A comfortable arrangement. In fact, it was one of the Beverley girls, Rachel, who brought their plight to my attention.'

'You became quickly on calling terms with the Beverleys.'

'It was by accident. I found Miss Rachel rowing my children about the lake.'

'At Mannerling?'

'Yes, ma'am.'

'But she was not there by invitation?'

'No, but Mannerling is her former home, so I could not really chastise her for trespass.'

'I have something I must tell you,' said Lady Evans. 'The daughter of friends of mine, Prudence Makepeace, was here on a visit. I had hoped to make a match of it for her with Lord Burfield, but he was tricked and ensnared by Abigail Beverley in a most degrading way.'

'You fascinate me. Go on.'

'Abigail is the twin of Rachel. Rachel was to marry Harry Devers, son of the previous owners of Mannerling. She took fright, and on the day of the wedding Abigail, who looks much like her, took her twin's place. But on her wedding night she took fright as well—or so she *says*—and ran away from him and was found in Lord Burfield's bed. The scandal! Of

29

course he had to marry her after that, which was more than any of those penurious, grasping Beverleys deserves. Miss Trumble is all that is excellent, but I want you to be on your guard against the Beverleys. They have but one aim in life—to reclaim Mannerling, and they do not care how low they stoop to do it.'

'They are all too young for me,' said Charles mildly.

'They are serpents all, and your years will not protect you from their wiles.'

'Good heavens!' exclaimed the general. 'Perhaps it would be better to make other arrangements for Beth and Mark.'

Charles Blackwood sat silent, his thin black brows drawn down. Then he said, 'If this Miss Trumble is such a precious pearl, such a lady, such an estimable governess, then what is she doing with this wicked family of Beverleys?'

'She is fallen on hard times, obviously, and must earn her bread somewhere.'

'But with a powerful patroness such as yourself, she could surely find a better position.'

'More tea, General?' Lady Evans refilled his cup. 'Ah well, truth to tell, she does seem unfortunately attached to them. Perhaps she feels if she abandoned them they might end up on the streets.'

Charles's face darkened. 'I feel you go too far, Lady Evans. From what I have seen of the

Beverley sisters, they appear high-spirited but I would not describe them as sluts.'

'Let us talk about something else,' said Lady Evans. 'The subject depresses me. So how goes the world, General?'

The general talked about mutual friends and after a while he and his son rose to take their leave.

'So what did you think of all that, my boy?' demanded the general as their carriage rolled out through the gates of Hursley Park.

'About the Beverley girls? I do not know. But it is very simple to clear up the matter. I will ask Miss Trumble.'

'What! The governess? Remember your position, Charles.'

'You will come with me as well. Miss Trumble is not in the common way.'

*　　*　　*

When they approached Brookfield House, they could hear sounds of laughter from the garden. As they drew nearer, they saw the Beverley sisters and Mark and Beth playing a noisy game of blind-man's buff in the garden. Little Beth had a scarf over her eyes and was tottering this way and that, trying to catch one of them.

Charles felt a stab of conscience. He realized he could not remember the last time he had heard his children laugh. He dismounted from the carriage and scooped Beth up into his arms. He removed the blindfold and she cried, 'Papa!' and threw her chubby arms about his neck.

'Enjoying your studies?' he asked, seeing Miss Trumble rise from a chair at the corner of the lawn and walk towards them.

'Oh, Papa, we are having such larks,' said Beth.

He set her down on her feet. 'Then run along and have more larks. I wish to talk to Miss Trumble. A word with you in private, if you please, Miss Trumble.'

She curtsied and led the way back into the house. When they were in the parlour, Charles introduced his father.

The general surveyed this governess curiously. Although he judged her to be as old as he was himself, she carried herself with a sort of youthful grace. The brown curls under her lace cap did not show any signs of grey and her eyes in her lined face were large and sparkling.

'We have been on a call to Lady Evans,' began Charles, after they were seated.

'How does Lady Evans go on?'

'Very well, Miss Trumble, and desirous of a call from you.'

'It would hardly be fitting,' said Miss Trumble equably, 'for a woman in my position to call on Lady Evans.'

'Lady Evans appeared to think very highly of you.'

She bowed her head.

'Warned us against those Beverley girls,' put in the general bluntly.

'Oh, dear. Lady Evans has reason. She was desirous to make a marriage between a young lady, a Prudence Makepeace, and Lord Burfield, but Lord Burfield married Abigail Beverley.'

'This is awkward,' said Charles. 'But Lady Evans did alarm us by telling us about how that proposal was brought about.'

'Did she also tell you that Lord Burfield was and is deeply in love with Abigail? No, I thought not. Sirs, you must have heard the scandal. Prudence Makepeace had to flee the country after conspiring with Harry Devers to abduct Abigail on the day of her wedding to Lord Burfield.'

'We must have been abroad at the time,' said Charles.

'You were also not told,' went on Miss Trumble, 'that burning ambition to reclaim Mannerling was at the root of the Beverleys' schemes. They no longer harbour such ambitions. But do you blame them?'

'Well, yes,' said the general, amazed. 'Very unwomanly.'

'Exactly. Had they been men, you would have found their ambition laudable. Think on it, gentlemen. How many men do you know in society who have married heiresses to save their estates and not one breath of scandal sticks to their name? You must not be anxious. There will be nothing in their behaviour to alarm you. I promise you that. If, on the other hand, you do not trust me, then you must take your children away.'

A burst of happy laughter sounded from the garden.

'No,' said Charles slowly. 'I am too old for any of the Beverleys in any case. Is Lady Beverley not at home?'

'My mistress is indisposed. Lady Beverley is often indisposed.'

'I was going to invite the Beverleys to Mannerling, but if Lady Beverley is unwell...'

A gleam of mischief shone in the governess's eyes. 'Should you issue such an invitation, then it would go a long way to restoring her ladyship to health.'

Charles smiled. 'Shall we say tomorrow? You could all come to Mannerling in the carriage with the children.'

'I am sure they will accept. If you will excuse me, gentlemen, I shall go to see if Lady Beverley considers herself fit.'

'Fine lady, that,' said the general when the door closed behind Miss Trumble.

'Very fine,' agreed his son. 'Too fine to be a governess. Miss Trumble has the air of a duchess.'

'And what must we think of the girls now?'

'Harmless. Only dangerous if my heart was in danger, and you alone know that is hardly

34

ever to be the case again.'

'Poor Sarah,' said the general. Sarah was the late Mrs. Blackwood. 'She seemed such a merry little thing.'

'Too merry to confine her attentions to her husband,' said Charles harshly.

'Well, well, I always did have a soft spot for little Sarah. And she is dead now. Water under the bridge.'

Charles reflected that 'water under the bridge' was too trite a phrase to describe his fury and heartache when he found his wife had been unfaithful to him with the first footman.

'Shh,' he admonished. 'I hear our governess returning.' Both men stood up.

Miss Trumble entered and said demurely that Lady Beverley thanked them for their invitation and would be pleased to attend.

'Restored to health, hey?' demanded the general with a twinkle in his eye.

'Oh, yes, your kind invitation was very beneficial.'

'I say,' said the general as they moved to the door, 'come as well.'

Miss Trumble curtsied with grace. 'You are too kind.'

'There now,' said the general in high humour, 'got to keep my grandchildren in line, what?'

Miss Trumble smiled and led the way out to the garden.

Charles paused for a moment on the

threshold. Rachel was throwing a ball to Mark. Her fair hair gleamed in the sunlight. It had escaped from its pins and was tumbling about her shoulders. Her face was pink and her large blue eyes shone with laughter. He felt a tug at his heart and then gave a rueful smile. He hoped he was not going to start lusting after young girls at his age!

*   *   *

The next day Miss Trumble found herself left to school and entertain the Blackwood children on her own. The Beverley sisters were preparing for their visit to Mannerling. It saddened her that they should betray so much hectic excitement. Would that wretched house which appeared to have a malignant life of its own ever let them go?

Now that Mark and Beth were at ease with her after their first day of drawing and games, she began formal lessons, enjoying the quick intelligence they showed.

'You have done very well,' she said at last. 'Now I will read you a story.'

'Not one with ghosts in it,' said Mark.

'No ghosts. You are not afraid of ghosts, are you, Mark?'

His expressive little face turned a trifle pale, and he nodded.

'Come here and sit by me. You have seen a ghost?'

36

Again that little nod.

'At Mannerling?'

His small hand slid into hers for comfort. He gulped and nodded again.

'And what did this ghost look like?' Miss Trumble never jeered at the fears of children.

'Foxy,' whispered Mark. 'Sandy hair and green eyes.'

Miss Trumble felt cold. Judd had looked like that. 'There is a picture of a man in the Long Gallery who looks like that.'

'He was in my room,' said Mark in a low voice.

Miss Trumble's gaze sharpened. 'Do you mean he was clear, like a real person?'

'Oh, yes.'

'Have you told your father of this?'

'No, miss I have not been in the way of talking to him.'

'I think we both should say something. Now, I will read you a story about pirates.'

His face brightened and he went to sit beside his sister again. As Miss Trumble read the words of the story, her mind raced. She remembered her own fear when that chandelier on which Judd had hanged himself had started to revolve slowly, just as if there were a body hanging from it, and there had been no wind that day. And yet a real-life ghost that this little boy had been able to see and to describe! She could not believe it.

She finished reading, promising to read

more the following day, and sent the children out to play in the garden. Then she went in search of Barry Wort.

'Such excitement,' said Barry, tossing a bunch of weeds into a wheelbarrow. 'You would think they had Mannerling back again, the way they are going on.'

'I am beginning to regret not moving to Mannerling to look after those children.'

'You, miss? You would never desert us!'

'It is tempting. Let me tell you. The boy, Mark, swears he has seen the ghost of Judd.'

'Could it be, miss, because the boy was frightened and unhappy with that governess? Children do be very fanciful.'

'No, Barry, I do not think it is fancy in this case. If he had talked of a spectral figure or anything that sounded like a Gothic romance, I would have put it down to imagination. But he saw a real figure. Do you think perhaps that someone is playing a nasty trick on him?'

'With your permission, miss, and that of Mr. Blackwood, I would suggest that maybe I spend a few nights with the boy, on guard, so to speak.'

Miss Trumble smiled. 'What would I do without you?' Barry coloured with pleasure. 'You are always so sensible. I will discuss the matter with Mr. Blackwood.'

* * *

Two carriages from Mannerling arrived. Miss

Trumble and the children went in the smaller one and Lady Beverley and her daughters in the larger. Lady Beverley was showing no signs of illness and was dressed in a modish gown of blue silk with darker-blue velvet stripes and a bonnet embellished with dyed ostrich plumes. Rachel noticed that her mother had adopted the haughty, grand manner she had shown when she was mistress of Mannerling and wondered uneasily if Lady Beverley considered Charles Blackwood as a possible husband for one of her daughters.

Rachel was wearing a blue muslin gown which matched the colour of her eyes. It was high-waisted and puff-sleeved and had three deep flounces at the hem. But she considered that Belinda with her black curls and pink gown looked prettier and wondered whether Belinda really meant to set her cap at Charles Blackwood and in the same moment persuaded herself she did not care.

Soon they arrived at the tall iron gates of Mannerling. The lodge-keeper sprang to open them. He was a new face to the Beverleys. Lady Beverley insisted on telling the carriage to stop while she lowered the glass and quizzed the lodge-keeper in a high autocratic voice as to whether he was happy in his new employ. Rachel's heart sank. She privately hoped this would turn out to be the first of many visits, but if Lady Beverley started ordering around the Mannerling servants and criticizing any changes to the house, as she had done in the past, then Rachel feared this might prove to be their first and last visit.

She felt a tug at her heart as the great house came into view, its graceful wings springing out, as they had always done, from the central block of warm stone.

Then down from the carriage and into the hall, where the great chandelier glittered above their heads, and up the double staircase behind the stiff back of a correct butler.

'Remember your place, Miss Trumble,' hissed Lady Beverley, 'and sit in a corner of the room.'

Miss Trumble smiled vaguely but made no reply.

The general and his son rose at their entrance. Rachel was struck afresh by how handsome Charles looked with his black hair and odd green eyes. His legs were superb. She suddenly blushed as if he could read her naughty thoughts.

Miss Trumble curtsied and moved to a chair by the window.

'Miss Trumble,' cried the general. ' 'Pon rep, you must not hide yourself. Come and sit by me.' He patted the cushion on the sofa beside him.

Lady Beverley's pale eyes shone with an unlovely light but she refrained from saying anything.

'So what do you think of the place, hey?' the

40

general asked Miss Trumble. 'Many changes since your day?'

Lady Beverley found her voice. 'Miss Trumble was never at Mannerling,' she said. 'She came to us after The Fall.' By this she somehow implied that Miss Trumble was part of the Beverleys' loss of fortune and face.

'The Fall?' asked the general curiously.

'We were once one of the most powerful families in the land,' said Lady Beverley. 'My poor husband incurred debts and so we were driven from Mannerling, from our rightful home.' She took a wisp of handkerchief and dabbed her eyes.

There followed an awkward silence. Then Belinda said brightly and loudly, 'I see the pianoforte there and Lizzie has come along in her studies. Do play us something, Lizzie.'

Lizzie rose obediently, having been schooled by Miss Trumble that when asked to play, she should do so without forcing anyone to persuade her.

Soon Lizzie's fingers were rippling expertly over the keys. When she had finished playing a brisk rondo, the general begged her to play the tune of a popular ballad. Miss Trumble's end of the sofa where she was seated was next to Charles Blackwood's armchair. She leaned forward and said gently, 'I would like a word with you in private, sir.'

'Gladly. Come with me.' They both rose and under the curious eyes of the others left the room together. He led her into the small drawing-room, used by the Beverley sisters on rainy days when Mannerling had been their home.

'Now what is this all about?' he asked.

'I am worried about Mark.'

'What's amiss? Is he slow to learn?'

'Not at all. He has a quick intelligence.'

'Then what can it be?'

'He has seen a ghost—a ghost at Mannerling.'

'I hope I have not been mistaken in you, Miss Trumble,' said Charles gravely. 'All children usually have such fancies, and they should not be encouraged in indulging them.'

'I am not in the way of indulging children's fancies,' said Miss Trumble so sharply and with such an air of hauteur that Charles immediately felt like a naughty child himself.

'Forgive me. Explain.'

'Mark has given me a graphic description of Mr. Judd, one of the previous owners who hanged himself. He claims to have seen him. Had I really believed he had seen a ghost, or rather, had I thought that the boy thought he had seen a ghost, I would have done all in my power to reassure him and to talk him out of his fancies. The thing that troubles me is that I have an uneasy feeling that Mark may have seen a real person.'

He looked at her in amazement and then said, 'But why? Why would anyone try to frighten a child? We have no enemies.'

'I really do not know. I may be wrong. But to make sure, our odd man, Barry Wort, has offered to guard the boy's room. He is a strong and honest man. He is not of the Mannerling staff. With your permission, I will smuggle him up the back stairs this evening. I told him to call.'

'Very well.' He looked at her doubtfully. 'And how long is this experiment to go on?'

'A few nights, that is all.'

'I will have a truckle-bed set up in Mark's room.'

'Not by your servants,' said Miss Trumble quickly.

'You suspect my servants? They would not dare.'

'Humour me, Mr. Blackwood.'

'Oh, very well. I will attend to the matter myself.' He rang the bell. John, the footman, answered the summons. 'Fetch my son here,' ordered Charles.

After a few minutes, Mark appeared.

Charles studied the boy's expressive and sensitive face, feeling a pang that he had never really tried to get to know his own son.

'Sit down, Mark,' he said gently.

'A moment.' Miss Trumble moved quickly to the door and jerked it open. John was standing outside.

'Go about your business,' said Miss Trumble.

'I was simply waiting at hand to see whether the master wished any refreshments,' said John huffily.

'The master does not. Go away.'

She waited until John had gone off down the stairs, his liveried back stiff with outrage.

She closed the heavy door and then sat down.

'Mark,' began Charles, 'what is all this about a ghost?'

The boy threw a reproachful look at Miss Trumble.

'I am not usually in the way of betraying confidences,' said the governess. 'But I think this ghost of yours is something to be taken seriously. You father will not laugh at you.'

'Tell me about it,' said Charles.

'It happens sometimes during the night,' said Mark in a rush. 'He stands at the end of my bed and he is a foxy man with sandy hair and green eyes.'

'If it was night-time and dark, how were you able to see him so clearly?' asked Charles.

'The first time it was just a black figure,' said Mark. 'So I left a candle burning after that. Miss Terry found out and whipped me for burning the candle, but I was more afraid of the ghost than I was of her.'

'See here, Mark,' said his father, 'we are going to play a game. Do you know ... er ... what is the name of the Brookfield servant?'

'Barry Wort.'

'Oh, I know him. He is capital. He taught me how to make a sling.'

'Now this is to be our secret, Mark,' said Charles. 'This Barry Wort is going to sleep in your room for a few nights. You are not to tell anyone about this arrangement, not the servants, not anyone.'

The boy's eyes shone. 'No ghost would dare to appear if Barry were there.'

'We shall see. I shall call on you before you go to sleep. Is there still a truckle-bed in the powder-closet in your room?'

Mark nodded.

'So take some sheets and blankets from the linen-press when the servants are not around and make a bed for Barry.'

'In the powder-closet?'

'No, that would not serve. In the corner of your room. You may leave now.'

Mark rose and bowed and walked to the door. Then he turned and ran back and threw his arms around the startled Miss Trumble's neck and deposited a wet kiss on her cheek. 'Thank you,' he whispered. And then he ran out.

'Shall we return to the company?' asked Charles stiffly. His conscience was hurting him. To see his own son run with gratitude to a stranger had shown him how very afraid and ill-treated the boy must have been.

They returned to the drawing-room in time to hear dinner being announced. Lady

Beverley rose and shook out her skirts. 'I am sure the servants' hall will provide you with something, Miss Trumble,' she said.

'Can't have that,' exclaimed the general. 'Told Miss Trumble to come. Guest.'

'How very kind,' said Lady Beverley with a thin smile. 'Your arm, General. It is such a long time since I have been on the arm of such an *attractive* gentleman.'

Rachel cast a covert look at Miss Trumble and she in her turn took Charles's arm and Miss Trumble gazed blandly back before slipping away to guide Barry into the house.

What is Mama about, to behave so stupidly? wondered Rachel, as Lady Beverley flirted with the general over dinner.

The general tried to address several remarks to Miss Trumble, but Lady Beverley treated each remark as if it had been addressed to herself.

And then Rachel surprised a mocking, rather speculative look on Charles Blackwood's face as he looked at her mother. Then he said, 'I had the pleasure of calling on an old friend, Lady Evans. You are acquainted with her, I believe?'

'We have had that pleasure,' said Lady Beverley and then remained comparatively silent for the rest of the meal.

So that was it, thought Rachel. He had heard of the vulgar, ambitious Beverleys, and although he thought his own age saved him from being a target, the mother had decided to set her cap at his father. Rachel felt herself blush with shame, her appetite fled and she picked at the food on her plate.

Her mother is embarrassing her dreadfully, thought Charles. He set himself to talk to her, asking her many questions about the neighbourhood and about the market town of Hedgefield until he felt her begin to relax.

'What did Miss Trumble wish to speak to you about?' she asked finally.

'Something to do with Mark's education,' he said. 'But you must ask her if you wish to know more.'

'I do not know what we would do without our Miss Trumble,' said Rachel with a little sigh.

'You should soon be making your come-out,' he said.

'My sister, Abigail, Lady Burfield, has invited me to London.'

'And when do you go?'

'To tell the truth, I have not made up my mind.'

'But why? A young lady like yourself should be enjoying balls and parties.'

'We have balls here in the country.'

'Ah, the local assembly. But can it compete with Almack's?'

She smiled. 'I have not known much of the grand life of late. I should probably feel sadly out of place and provincial.'

'With your appearance and Miss Trumble's schooling, I do not think you have anything to fear.'

And Rachel, who would have accepted such a compliment with flirtatious ease before the revelation that he had called on Lady Evans, found all she could do was stare at her plate and wish the dinner-party were over.

After dinner, the general suggested they promenade in the Long Gallery. 'I see you have placed the portraits of yourself, your son and your own ancestors here,' exclaimed Miss Trumble.

'Why not?' demanded Charles Blackwood crossly. 'You could hardly expect us to hang the Beverleys. They are in the attics, I believe.'

'I meant that there is no portrait of Judd,' said Miss Trumble quietly.

Rachel saw Charles look at Miss Trumble with dawning realization on his face. So little Mark must have confided in his father and governess about the sighting of that ghost. Rachel herself had assumed the boy had seen that portrait and his imagination had done the rest. But perhaps he had been in the attics. Children loved poking around in attics.

'As to your ancestors,' said Charles, turning to Lady Beverley, 'I cannot understand why the previous owners held on to them. If you wish, I will send them over in a fourgon tomorrow.'

'That will not be necessary,' said Lady

Beverley. She raised her quizzing-glass to study a portrait of the general.

'May I ask why? I thought you would be delighted to have them back.'

'They belong at Mannerling,' said Lady Beverley.

There must be something about this place that deranges people, thought Charles. I am glad I have not felt it. To him, on first viewing the property, it had seemed peaceful and beautiful with its great hall and painted ceilings.

They moved to the Green Saloon, where the general promptly sat next to Miss Trumble and engaged her in conversation until Lady Beverley could not bear it any longer. She raised her voice. 'Miss Trumble! I have left my fan in the carriage. Pray be so good as to fetch it.'

'Your fan is on your wrist,' said Rachel sharply.

'Oh, so it is. You have some pretty pieces and ornaments here, General. Do tell me how you came by them.'

'Here and there. I am not the artistic one. You must ask my son.' And the general turned his attention back to Miss Trumble.

Lady Beverley fell silent while her mind worked busily. She must get rid of this governess who was taking up so much of the general's attention. But if she gave her her marching orders, then Miss Trumble would simply move to Mannerling. How dare Miss Trumble adopt the manners and attitudes of a duchess. She simply did not know her place. Hitherto Lady Beverley had been too grateful to have a governess so cheaply that she had not wondered overmuch why Miss Trumble's promised references had never arrived. Her eyes sharpened. There must be some mystery. There was something in Miss Trumble's past that lady did not want her to find out. She would demand those references and then write to previous employers and then she would know all.

The evening came to an end. The Beverley sisters were very subdued. Belinda was so ashamed of her mother's behaviour that she had made no attempt to flirt with Charles. Rachel looked awkward and uncomfortable and kept looking at the clock, as if she thought the evening would never end.

So much for the scheming Beverleys, mused Charles ruefully. The sisters were certainly not interested in engaging his attentions, and Rachel almost seemed to find him a bore!

At last Lady Beverley announced they must leave. She could hardly wait until they were home so that she could confront Miss Trumble.

She did not know that the shrewd governess had anticipated the summons and was already making plans, so that, when Lady Beverley asked her for a word in private, Miss Trumble acquiesced with every appearance of calm, a calm that did not desert her when Lady Beverley said she must now insist on seeing those references.

'I will arrange for them to be sent directly,' said Miss Trumble. 'But why this sudden concern, my lady?'

Lady Beverley paced up and down the room, showing no sign of the recent ill health she had claimed to have suffered from.

'The reason is,' she said haughtily, 'although I consider it impertinent in you to ask my reasons, that because of your position in this household you are tutoring the Mannerling children. It is up to me to make sure you have perfect references should the general ask to see them.'

And all that translated into, thought Miss Trumble, is that you see a chance of marrying the general and do not want me to get in the way and you are hoping to find some fault in my past and therefore have a reason for dismissing me.

Miss Trumble curtsied. 'Will that be all, my lady?'

Lady Beverley looked at her, baffled. She had been hoping for some sign of worry or distress. 'That will be all,' she said grandly.

Miss Trumble paused in the doorway. 'Perhaps I should mention one little thing.'

'Go on.'

'Now that the Mannerling children are here

every weekday and dine with us, perhaps the food supplied could be more appropriate fare for the children of Mannerling.'

'The food is good and nourishing.'

'I heard Mark telling his grandfather that he had sat down to rook-pie for the first time. I just thought I would mention it.'

Miss Trumble smiled sweetly and left, closing the door very quietly behind her.

Lady Beverley could not know her governess had been lying and that Mark had said nothing of the kind. She turned pink at the idea that the Blackwoods might think her parsimonious or, worse, poor. Josiah, the cook, must be ordered to spend more money on his cooking.

Lady Beverley thought about getting out the accounts books to see if the extra money required could be pared from some other household expense but she caught the reflection of her face in the mirror over the fireplace. She thought she looked faded and tired. Lady Beverley had once been a great beauty, but lines of petulance, added to the lines of age, had given her face a crumpled look. She must start using proper washes and lotions. Her hand reached for the bell. Miss Trumble would know what to do. Then she hesitated. With any luck, Miss Trumble would soon not be around for very much longer, so it was better to get used to doing without her.

In her room, Miss Trumble sat down before

her travelling writing-desk and began to write busily. While she wrote, she decided to call on Lady Evans the following day.

*   *   *

'Letitia!' exclaimed Lady Evans the following afternoon as Miss Trumble was ushered into the drawing-room of Hursley Park by the butler.

'You look a trifle guilty,' said Miss Trumble, stripping off her gloves, 'as well you should.'

'What can you mean, my dear? Come, be seated and tell me your news.'

'My news is that General Blackwood and his son Charles called on you and you saw fit to warn them against the Beverleys. Considering the totally criminal behaviour of your little friend, Prudence Makepeace, I am surprised at you.'

'You must admit, Abigail Beverley's behaviour in snaring Lord Burfield was disgraceful.'

'The thing you will not admit is that Burfield was and is madly in love with Abigail.'

'Pooh, love is all a fancy.'

'It seems to me that you must think so. I, on the other hand, love my charges dearly and do not want anything, or any malicious gossip, to stand in their way.'

Lady Evans bridled. ' "Malicious" is too strong a word. The general is an old friend.

Even you must admit, Letitia, that the Beverleys have been guilty of blatant plotting and manipulation to regain Mannerling.'

Miss Trumble gave a little sigh. 'That is in the past.'

'And so it should be. Charles Blackwood is too old for any of them. Come, let us not quarrel. I swear I will not say a word against the wretched girls again. There. You have my promise. Are you still bent on keeping on such a demeaning job, one which is well below your position in life?'

'No one knows about me except you, and no one must.'

'Oh, very well. But it is all very strange.'

'Lady Beverley is demanding my references.'

'Awkward. Do you want one from me?'

'No, I have written to several ladies who will supply me with the necessary letters.'

'Why should she ask for them now?'

'I do not know,' lied Miss Trumble, who had no intention of telling Lady Evans that Lady Beverley was setting her cap at the general and did not want competition.

'I saw you arrive and driving yourself! Where is that servant, Barry?'

'Oh, he is on an errand,' said Miss Trumble vaguely, and then began to wonder again how Barry was getting on.

*　　　*　　　*

Barry was bored. He had slipped down the

back stairs and had hidden in the grounds while the maids came in during the morning to clean the boy's room. He planned to creep back when the coast was clear and get some much-needed sleep, for he had been awake all night long, without the sign of a ghost or even hearing a creaking floor-board.

He wandered over in the direction of the lake and went and sat in the folly, smoked his pipe, and admired the view. If there was no sign of the ghost the next night, he would beg leave to return to his duties at Brookfield House.

When he finally decided it was safe to return, he strolled back by a circuitous route, keeping all the while out of sight of the many windows of Mannerling. Then he sprinted out of the shelter of some concealing shrubbery and ran for the back door. If any servant surprised him on the stairs, he would say he had a letter to deliver to Mr. Charles Blackwood personally. With a sigh of relief, he gained Mark's bedchamber, drew the truckle-bed out from its hiding place in the closet, lay on top of it, fully dressed, and fell promptly into a deep sleep.

He was awakened in the early evening by Mark leaping on top of him and crying, 'Wake up. Miss Trumble read us some more about pirates. We could play pirates on the lake. Please!'

'Keep your voice down, young man. I'm not supposed to be here.'

The door opened and Charles Blackwood

came in carrying a tray of food and a tankard of beer. 'You must be very hungry,' he said ruefully to Barry. 'I had forgot you could not even go to the kitchens.'

Barry scrambled to his feet and gratefully took the tray. 'I do be sharp set, sir. Most good of you.'

'Papa,' pleaded Mark, 'I learned all about pirates today and would like Barry to come to the lake and play with me.'

'And what about this ghost?'

'Oh,' said Mark in a disappointed little voice. 'Perhaps I imagined it.'

'We'll see,' said Charles. 'One more night and then we will review the situation. You may go and play with Beth and leave your guard here to enjoy his meal in peace.'

Mark ran off. 'Do you think he imagined the ghost, sir?' ventured Barry.

'He described his ghost most vividly. As I said, we will try again tonight.'

Charles left and Barry settled down to enjoy his meal in peace, noticing that Charles had made sure there was enough food for a very hungry man. Barry did not want to see any of the Beverley girls ever again plotting and scheming to get back to Mannerling, but there was no denying Mr. Blackwood was a fine-looking man. He must have married late, for the children were young. He wondered what the late Mrs. Blackwood had been like.

*   *   *

Back at Brookfield House, Rachel was wondering the same thing aloud as she sat with Miss Trumble in the parlour. 'For it suddenly occurred to me that there were portraits of Mr. Blackwood and his father in the Long Gallery and a charming portrait of the children, but no portrait of Mrs. Blackwood, although there was one of the general's wife. There were various portraits of ladies but in such old-fashioned gowns that they must have been the ancestors.'

'Well, unless he volunteers to tell us about her, we can hardly ask him,' said Miss Trumble. She herself had forgotten to ask Lady Evans about the late Mrs. Blackwood. The governess looked speculatively at Rachel. 'Mr. Charles Blackwood is a good man and his children are delightful. If he ever marries again, I would hope it would be for love.'

Rachel sighed. 'Apart from my lucky elder sisters, love does not seem to enter into fashionable marriages.'

'Better to make an unfashionable marriage than a loveless one.'

Rachel smiled. 'I would have thought a sensible lady like yourself would not have believed in love in a cottage.'

'It need not be a cottage. Anywhere but Mannerling, in fact.'

Lady Beverley came in at that moment, a

57

letter in her hand. 'Such news,' she said. 'I had this letter from Isabella this morning, but did not read it all until now. She is returning with her husband to Perival.' Perival was Viscount Fitzpatrick's, Isabella's husband's, English estate, which lay near them on the other side of Mannerling.

'Splendid!' cried Rachel, elated at the news of the return of the eldest Beverley sister. 'Does Mrs. Kennedy accompany them?' Mrs. Kennedy was the viscount's aunt.

'That hurly-burly Irishwoman! I trust not,' said Lady Beverley. 'Mrs. Kennedy was a vulgar influence on you girls.'

'How can you say that, Mama? Mrs. Kennedy was kindness itself.'

'In any case, Isabella says nothing of her.'

'When do they plan to arrive?' asked Miss Trumble.

'In a month's time.'

Rachel slipped out of the room and went in search of Belinda and Lizzie to tell them the great news.

Lizzie clapped her hands. 'We will see our nephew and niece. Let me see, Margaret must be two, and Guy, three years old. Have you told Barry? He was always monstrous fond of Isabella.'

'I cannot find Barry. Where is he?'

'All Miss Trumble will say is that he has gone off on an errand, but whatever errand it was, it has taken him away for quite some time.'

*   *   *

Barry stifled a yawn and sat up on the truckle-bed. Better to get up and sit on a chair in case he fell asleep. It was so tempting to close his eyes. Mark had been a cheerful and happy child before he fell asleep. Barry was sure that this ghost did not exist.

He had left the shutters on one window open, and a shaft of moonlight fell across the boards of the floor. Mark's little bed was a modern one with a canopy, rather than a four-poster with curtains that could be drawn round it in the night, which was why he could claim to have seen a ghost standing at the end of his bed.

Barry's eyelids began to droop. He had not managed to have enough sleep during the day.

And then those eyes jerked open. He heard a soft shuffling movement in the corridor outside. He felt on the floor beside him for his stout cudgel and tensed, waiting.

The door slowly swung open. The corridor outside was in darkness but he could dimly make out a tall figure standing in the doorway, a thicker piece of darkness.

The figure walked forwards and stood at the end of the bed. Barry had told Mark not to light a candle.

Barry fought down a sudden superstitious feeling of pure panic.

Then he heard the scrape of a tinder-box. The figure had moved to the side of the bed and was lighting a candle.

Barry's moment of panic fled. Ghosts, Barry thought firmly, easing himself to his feet, did not light candles.

But as the little flame sprang up, he suppressed a gasp. Surely this was Judd. He was dressed all in black, with a long black cloak, but the hair was sandy and the foxy features were familiar.

'What are you doing here?' shouted Barry.

The figure swung to face him and at the same time raised his cloak to hide his face and let out a sepulchral moan. Mark started up and began to scream.

The 'ghost' made for the door. 'I'll give you something to moan about,' cried Barry and lashed out with his cudgel.

The man ducked and the cudgel caught him a glancing blow on the side of the head. He fell heavily, but quickly rallied and staggered out into the corridor. Barry stumbled over one of Mark's toys and fell headlong. He scrambled back to his feet and ran out into the corridor. But the 'ghost' had gone. Barry ran through the corridors of the great house, shouting and yelling. Cries came from the downstairs, where sleepy servants, roused from their beds by the noise, stumbled out into the great hall.

Charles Blackwood appeared wrapped in a magnificent silk banyan. 'What is it, Barry?'

'The ghost,' said Barry. 'I struck him a blow on the head but then I fell over something on the bedroom floor and he got away.'

'So the boy was telling the truth.'

Charles ran down to the hall and gave orders to the servants. For the rest of the night the house was searched from top to bottom, and the gamekeepers, grooms, and gardeners searched the grounds.

At last they met again in the dawn light, all gathered in the hall.

Charles addressed them. 'Someone has been trying to frighten my son. If any of you is responsible, then I shall take you personally to the nearest round-house. I want two guards to be on duty from now on outside my son's door at night.'

He did not want any of the newly hired Mannerling servants. He had not chosen any of his own he had brought with him for fear they, too, would gossip. But he now realized that they would never be part of any plot to harm his son. He selected one groom and one stablehand and gave them their orders. They had been in his employ for some time and appeared to be trustworthy.

He then turned to Barry. 'You have done well. I doubt if our ghost will materialize again.' He handed Barry two guineas, which Barry swiftly pocketed.

The odd man said he would walk back to Brookfield House, as the morning was fine. He felt very tired. But something was nagging at the back of his mind. He had scanned the servants' faces when they were gathered in the hall, looking for anyone with the same type of features as Judd, but he could not see one. It suddenly struck him that there was one face that should have been among the crowd, a face that was absent.

He was still mulling it over as he walked up the short drive to Brookfield House. He walked round the side of the building and round the back to the kitchen door. He was reaching up his hand to the latch when the door suddenly opened and Miss Trumble stood there.

'What news, Barry? I had a restless night and rose early. I saw you arrive.'

'I chased the ghost.' Barry described what had happened.

'But who would do such a thing, and why?'

'That I do not know, miss, but there do be something troubling me. When we was all gathered in the hall, all the servants, indoor and outdoor, I looked round the faces to see if I could spot anyone who might have tried to dress up as Judd, someone who looked a bit like him, but I couldn't see anyone. Then, as I was walking back home, I came to the conclusion that someone was missing out o' that gathering, but I couldn't guess who it could be.'

'John,' said Miss Trumble bleakly.

'John?'

'The footman. He is tall and thin. His eyes are pale green. He could have worn a sandy wig.'

Barry scratched his head in perplexity. 'But John is a milk-sop, a cringing, mincing man-milliner.'

'Forget his character and try to imagine him in a sandy wig.'

'Could be,' said Barry reluctantly. 'What should we do?'

'If you are not too tired, hitch up the carriage and we will go back to Mannerling. You say you struck John.'

'Twas but a glancing blow, miss.'

'Nonetheless, his head must be examined and his quarters searched.'

'I'll get the carriage right away.'

*　　*　　*

Charles Blackwood, roused from a late sleep, heard their suspicions. 'You did right to come to me direct,' he said, cutting across the governess's apologies for having awakened him.

He rang the bell. A footman Miss Trumble did not know answered it promptly.

'Send the footman, John, to me,' commanded Charles. He turned to Miss Trumble and Barry. 'Now we shall see.'

After some moments, John appeared and

stood meekly before them.

'Come here,' ordered Charles, 'and kneel before me.'

John flashed a sudden look of venom at Miss Trumble, quickly veiled. He knelt in front of his master. Charles whipped off the footman's white wig and then felt carefully over his close-cropped head.

Then he replaced the wig and said, 'Stand.'

John did as he was bid. 'May I be so bold to ask what this is all about?' he asked.

'In a minute. After the search for this ghost, when the servants were all assembled in the hall, you were not there.'

'But I was, sir. I was standing at the back with Mrs. Jones, the housekeeper, and Freddy, the pot-boy.'

'Bring them here,' ordered Charles.

They waited in silence until the housekeeper and the pot-boy were brought in by John.

The housekeeper was small and stout, encased in black bombazine, keys at her waist and an enormous starched cap on her head. Her face had a high shiny glaze and her little eyes held a look of perpetual outrage.

Gin, thought Miss Trumble.

The pot-boy was undersized and had a loose wet mouth and moist black eyes. He gawked about him with bovine stupidity.

'John, here, says he was at the back of the Great Hall this morning at dawn after we had all given up the search for the man who tried to impersonate the late Mr. Judd. Is that the case? Was John with you?'

'Yes, sir,' said the housekeeper. She had a deep hoarse voice. Definitely gin, thought Miss Trumble.

'You are sure?'

'Oh, yes, sir. John says to me, he says, that it might have been a real ghost after all.'

'And you, boy?' said Charles to Freddy.

Freddy tugged his forelock. 'I seed 'im as plain as day, sir.'

He looked to the housekeeper for approval.

'You may go,' said Charles. 'Not you, John.'

When the housekeeper and pot-boy had left, Charles said, 'You are the only servant who could have impersonated the late Mr. Judd, because of your looks. But obviously I was mistaken. You may go about your duties. But remember and tell the other servants—if I find the culprit, I will deal with him first before I hand him over to the authorities.'

CHAPTER THREE

She likes her self, yet others hates
For that which in herself she prizes;
And, while she laughs at them, forgets
She is the thing that she despises.

WILLIAM CONGREVE

Somehow, the sisters had expected the excitement of a visit to Mannerling to go on forever. But rainy days set in and although the children came daily during the week, neither Charles nor his father came with them. There was only the local assembly to look forward to, and that, the sisters privately thought, would be the usual dull affair. Of course, Isabella would soon be with them and that was at least something exciting. But the damp dreary days made the hours drag by. Barry began to worry about getting them safely to the assembly and in an open carriage, too, for thick fog had started to shroud the countryside at night, along with the persistent drenching rain.

Lady Beverley was once more victim of one of her imaginary illnesses and demanded 'absolute quiet,' so there were not even Lizzie's tunes at the pianoforte to enliven their days. And then, just when it seemed to the sisters that they would be locked in this rainy, foggy, silent grave of Brookfield House forever, the day before the assembly the morning sun appeared and burnt through the fog, leaving the countryside glittering and shining under a clear blue sky.

And Mark and Beth arrived with a letter from the general to say he and his son would be at the assembly, for friends of theirs had come to stay at Mannerling and were anxious to sample the 'local excitements.'

Belinda and Lizzie took out gowns and feathers and lace. A party from Mannerling might include some young men!

Rachel said it would amuse her now to go and see all the ladies trying to ensnare the owner of Mannerling.

A package arrived in the mail for Miss Trumble. She opened it and took out several letters and read them with a smile. Then she went in search of Lady Beverley. Her mistress was up and about and looking over several gowns. 'What do you think I should wear, Miss Trumble?' she asked when she saw the governess. 'I wore this plum velvet for half-mourning, but I fear it looks sadly démodé.'

'There is a pale-blue silk here, very grand, and a good line,' said Miss Trumble, picking up the gown from the bed and shaking out the folds. 'With an overdress, the one you have, you know, of darker-blue sarsenet, 'twould be very fetching.'

'Perhaps you have the right of it.'

'My references, my lady.' Miss Trumble held them out.

'Put them on my desk over there, Oh, and Miss Trumble, it will not be necessary for you to accompany us. I do not like to leave the house empty.'

'The maids will be here, and Josiah.'

'Servants are not responsible people.' Lady Beverley crossed to the glass and studied her own reflection critically. 'I need you to prepare a pomade and one of your washes for my face, Miss Trumble.'

'Alas, I have mislaid my recipe book and fear I cannot.'

Both women eyed each other. Lady Beverley knew that the governess would now punish her for having been forbidden the assembly. There would be no more lotions, pomades, powders, washes, and, above all, magic draughts for those tiresome headaches.

'On the other hand,' said Lady Beverley, 'I suppose Josiah is protection enough for this poky little house. You may accompany us.'

'I do believe I left my book in the kitchen with Josiah. I will go directly and look for it.'

When the governess had left, Lady Beverley eagerly scanned those references. Her face fell. There were three letters, all from ladies of impeccable rank and lineage, and their praise for Miss Trumble was of the highest order.

Lady Beverley gave a petulant little shrug. What chance had a mere governess with such as the general? Such a man would not lower himself to wed a governess!

*　　*　　*

To the sisters' delight, their mother hired a closed carriage and coachman to drive them all to the assembly. The assembly, from being damned as a tiresome village affair, had become enchanted in their eyes because the owner of Mannerling was to be there.

Rachel did not want to arrive late but her mother did, Lady Beverley liking to make an entrance. She fondly imagined the general and his son being bored by the dismal country company and how their eyes would light up at the sight of the Beverley family.

Mary Judd was pinning up a stray lock of hair in the ante-room provided for the ladies when they arrived. Miss Trumble, resplendent in gold silk and with a Turkish turban to match on her pomaded curls, noticed that Mary's little black eyes were shining with malice and wondered why.

'Just arrived?' asked Rachel.

'No, I have been here this age,' said Mary. 'So passé to arrive late, do you not think?'

'I wouldn't know the ways of the world, any more than you,' retorted Rachel. 'Out with it, Mary. You eyes are full of secrets. Is the party from Mannerling here?'

'You will see for yourself.' Mary flitted out.

69

'I suppose Mr. Charles Blackwood has turned up with a beautiful lady and she thinks we will be disappointed,' said Lizzie, and they all laughed at the joke.

They could hear the jolly strains of the local band playing a country dance. The air was full of the smells of scent and pomade, wood-smoke, wine and beer. They pushed open the double doors which opened into the assembly room.

It was a long room at the side of the inn, with a fire burning at either end. The band played in a little gallery which over-looked the room. At first Rachel saw only familiar faces and then the crowd of watchers in front of her parted and she could see the whole ballroom.

In the centre of the room, his height topping the dancers, was Charles Blackwood, partnered by a very tall, very beautiful woman. Her hair was as fair as Rachel's and her eyes of a very intense blue. She had high cheek-bones, a long straight nose, and a statuesque figure, slim but deep-breasted, and she was nearly as tall as Charles Blackwood. She was wearing a gown of silver gauze over an underslip of white satin. Diamonds sparkled in her hair and round her perfect white neck.

Rachel stood there, feeling small and diminished. This Amazon was a sort of grander Rachel, taller, more assured, with bluer eyes and a sophisticated, commanding presence.

'Oh, dear,' whispered Lizzie. 'Who can she be?'

'I fear that is our Mr. Blackwood's house guest,' said Rachel. 'Perhaps her husband is here.'

'From the way she is looking at Mr. Blackwood and he at her,' said Belinda, 'I fear there is no husband.'

The general had seen them and came bustling up. 'Capital,' he exclaimed. 'You are looking very fine tonight, Miss Trumble.' Lady Beverley glared daggers. 'And you, too, dear lady,' said the general hastily. 'Ah, the dance is finishing. You must make the acquaintanceship of our guests.'

They followed him in a little group to where Charles was bowing before his partner at the end of the dance. 'Charles, my boy,' cried the general. 'They are come at last.'

Charles smiled at them. 'Lady Beverley, may I present my friend, Miss Minerva Santerton. Ah, and here is George, Mr. Santerton, Miss Santerton's brother.' He introduced brother and sister to the Beverleys and Miss Trumble. George Santerton was as tall as his sister, with the same fair hair, but his eyes were a washed-out blue and held a vacuous look and his chin receded into his high, starched cravat.

'Charmed,' he drawled. 'Didn't expect so many beauties at a little country dance.'

Minerva smiled, a small, curved smile. 'But you must have heard of the famous Beverley

71

sisters,' she said. 'Even I have heard of them. Your fame is known in London.'

Her voice hesitated a little before the word 'fame,' as if she had been about to say 'notoriety.'

Rachel felt a tug at her arm and found Mark looking up at her. 'May I have the next dance, Miss Rachel?'

Minerva smiled indulgently. 'Shall we find some refreshment, Charles, and leave the children to their dance?'

She put a proprietorial hand on his arm. A flash of irritation crossed Charles's green eyes, but he bowed and led her away.

Rachel performed a dance, another country one, with Mark, trying to remind herself that children always came to dances at these country assemblies, but feeling gauche and awkward and wishing she had a handsome partner to restore some of her wounded vanity. She and her sisters had been used to being the most beautiful women at any country affair and she felt their lustre had been sadly dimmed by this visiting goddess.

As if in answer to her wishes for a handsome partner, no sooner was the dance over and the supper dance announced than a gentleman was bowing before her. Rachel hesitated just a moment. She had expected to be led into supper after this dance by Charles. Perhaps, she thought furiously, if Mama had not arrived so late, there would have been time for Charles to have asked her. She realized the gentleman in front of her was looking at her quizzically and waiting for her reply.

She dropped a low curtsy and said, 'I am delighted, sir.'

And then she took a proper look at him. He was a stranger to the neighbourhood; she had not seen him before. He was of medium height with thick brown hair fashionably cut, which gleamed in the candle-light with red glints. His square, regular face was deeply tanned.

Suddenly mindful of the conventions, Rachel said, as he led her to the floor, 'We have not been introduced, sir.'

'I thought such conventions were only for London balls.'

'No, I assure you.'

He led her to the Master of Ceremonies, Squire Blaine, and said, 'Pray introduce me to this beautiful lady.'

'Certainly,' said the squire. 'Miss Beverley, may I present Mr. Hercules Cater, whom I met earlier today. Mr. Cater is a sugar planter from the Indies. Mr. Cater, the star of our county, Miss Rachel Beverley of Brookfield House.'

'There we are,' he said gaily, leading her to the centre of the floor. 'Now we are all that is respectable.'

The dance was a quadrille, which many people in the county still did not know how to perform, and so there was only one set: Rachel and Mr. Cater, Charles and Minerva, the

73

general and Lady Beverley, and Belinda and George Santerton.

It gladdened Rachel's heart to notice how ungracefully Minerva danced. Her own partner, Mr. Cater, danced with ease and grace, drawing applause from the audience by performing an entrechat, quite in the manner of the bon ton who employed ballet masters to teach them elaborate steps.

Miss Trumble watched the dancers. She was glad the general was dancing with Lady Beverley. For had the general chosen her, Miss Trumble, for the supper dance, then, the governess knew, her mistress would have done everything in her power to ruin the evening for everyone else.

And then she noticed Lady Evans sitting in a quiet corner and made her way there.

'Ah, Letitia,' said Lady Evans, who was wearing an enormous turban instead of one of her usual giant caps. 'Come and sit by me, for I am become bored.'

'You must not call me Letitia in public,' admonished Miss Trumble, sitting down beside her. 'If it bores you so much, why do you come?'

'Curiosity. I was anxious to see Miss Santerton with my own eyes. I have heard so much about her.'

'Indeed! I am so out of the world, I have heard nothing at all. How old is she, would you say?'

'I know her exact age. She is one of the Sussex Santertons. Good family. Minerva is twenty-eight.'

'So old, so beautiful, and not married! No money?'

'The Santertons are as rich as Croesus.'

'So what is the problem?'

'Minerva Santerton is a widow.'

'Then why is she called Santerton?'

'It is a dark story. She married Sir Giles Santerton, a first cousin. They were married only a little over a year when Sir Giles was found drowned in a pond on his estate. Now, he had been heard quarrelling with Minerva—evidently they fought like cat and dog—on the morning of the day he died. Also, when his body was pulled from the water, he had a lump the size of an egg on his head. There were a few nasty rumours.'

'Such as?'

'Such as that his wife had hit him on the head and pushed him to his death. But Giles's father was and is the local magistrate and shuddered at the idea of scandal, and he had not been overfond of his son in any case, and so nothing more was said about the whole business and the rumours died away. My friend, Mrs. Tullock, who knows the family and is of Sussex, went to the funeral and said Minerva cried most affectingly and even fainted at the graveside.'

'But she was introduced to the Beverleys as

Miss Santerton!'

'The death took place four years ago. After a period of mourning, Miss Santerton appeared once more on the social scene. She seems determined to be regarded as a débutante.'

'At her age, and apparently never having been married, she is in danger of being damned as an ape-leader.' Spinsters were still believed to be damned when they died to lead apes in hell.

'I think she is still in a way out for revenge on the dead Giles by acting as if the marriage never happened,' said Lady Evans.

'Why did she marry him if she hated him that much?'

'Her mother was dead and her father, considerably older than the mother, mark you, was an awful old tyrant. He arranged the marriage, he and Giles's father.'

'But a first cousin ...' protested Miss Trumble.

'Oh, they were married by a bishop, and one can always bribe a bishop. Now take that fellow dancing with Rachel. He is a Mr. Cater, a sugar planter, and said to be enormously wealthy. Good parti.'

'All these people arriving out of nowhere,' murmured Miss Trumble. 'And I had the stage so nicely set.'

'What's that, hey?'

'Nothing of importance,' said Miss Trumble sadly. 'Nothing important at all.'

Rachel found Mr. Cater pleasant company at supper. She judged him to be in his mid-twenties, certainly nearer her age than Charles Blackwood. 'And what brings you to Hedgefield?' she asked.

'Curiosity. I met someone out in the West Indies who spoke of the beauties of Mannerling, and finding time on my hands, I decided to travel into the country and perhaps see the place for myself.'

'Mannerling,' echoed Rachel, her face lighting up.

'You know the place well?'

'Of course; it was our family home until some years ago.' Her large eyes shone. 'It must be the most beautiful place in the world.'

'I have already spoken to the present owner, Mr. Charles Blackwood. He has kindly allowed me to visit Mannerling and see for myself.'

'Oh, it is so wonderful. Such an air of peace and elegance. I miss it so much. We were happy there. Who told you of Mannerling?'

'An elderly gentleman, Lord Hexhamworth.'

'Ah, yes, he was a friend of my father and was always invited to our balls. We had wonderful balls.'

'Mr. Blackwood seems much taken with Miss Santerton.'

Rachel looked down the long table to where Charles sat with Minerva.

'Yes,' she agreed, but impatiently. For some reason she wanted to forget the existence of Charles Blackwood and the glorious Minerva, who made her feel small and provincial. 'The last ball we had at Mannerling,' she went on, 'was the finest. The walls were draped with silk, and a double row of footmen lined the grand staircase, each man carrying a gold sword.'

'That is extravagance to rival the Prince Regent!'

'It was so very fine.' She gave a little sigh. 'But we have accepted our new life and are relatively happy.'

'Perhaps Mr. Blackwood can be persuaded to let *you* show me the delights of Mannerling.'

'That would not be fitting. Besides, I would feel like an interloper.'

'And yet your beauty in a beautiful house would surely be fitting.'

'Thank you, sir, for the compliment. Do you stay long in England?'

'Several months. I have not been home this age.'

'Tell me about your life in the Indies.'

At first she listened, fascinated, to the tales of hurricanes and heat, of hard labour and the rewards of being a plantation owner. But when he began to complain of the laziness of his black slaves, Rachel began to feel uncomfortable. Miss Trumble had lectured them on the evils of slavery. And yet she had up until that point found the company of this easygoing Mr. Cater pleasant.

'You obviously do not believe in all this talk of freedom for slaves,' she said at last.

Something flickered through the depths of his eyes and he said with a light laugh, 'It may seem brutal to you here, in your sheltered world of England. But you would soon change your views were you in the West Indies. Sugar must be harvested and white skins are not up to labouring in the sun.'

'Possibly,' agreed Rachel. 'But slaves!'

He smiled indulgently. 'You are a very modern young lady. But tell me more about Mannerling.'

And in her enthusiasm in describing her old home, Rachel forgot for the rest of the evening about those slaves.

*　　*　　*

Charles Blackwood had to admit to himself that he was becoming quickly fascinated by the beautiful Minerva. He had not invited either Minerva or her brother to stay; they had invited themselves. At first he had been irritated, for the acquaintanceship was slight and they had not asked if they could stay, had simply sent an express to say they would be arriving. George Santerton was a bore and a fool, but the glorious Minerva more than made

79

up for her brother's deficiencies.

The intense blue of her eyes, the gold of her hair, the swell of her bosom, and the way those magnificent eyes lit up with laughter went straight to his heart. He had planned never to marry again, but Minerva would make such a beautiful ornament in his beautiful home.

But there were Mark and Beth to consider before he even thought of presenting them with a new mother. His fury at his late wife's infidelity had made him neglect them. He realized that now and he was immensely grateful to Miss Rachel Beverley of Brookfield House for having brought that neglect to his attention. His eyes strayed to Rachel. She seemed to be enjoying the company of that stranger, Cater. If the man was as rich as rumour already had it, then perhaps yet another of the Beverley sisters would make a good marriage. He hoped she would find someone worthy of her. He could not in his heart blame the Beverleys for their reported machinations in trying to reclaim their home. The girls were very young and the plunge from riches to a sort of genteel straitened circumstances must have been hard. There was a soft glow about Rachel when she was happy that seemed to make Minerva's charms, by contrast, look like hard brilliance. He gave himself a mental shake. Minerva was speaking. 'I quite dote on your children,' she said. 'I feel it is a great tragedy that I have none of my own.'

'Perhaps you may yet have children,' he said lightly. 'You may marry again.'

'When one has made a bad mistake, or rather, one's father has forced one into an unhappy marriage, then one is not anxious to marry again.'

He looked at her with quick sympathy. 'I understand what you mean. But there are good people in this world.'

Her eyes caressed his face. 'I am beginning to think there are.'

He felt a little chill, a sense of withdrawal. Like all men, he wanted to be the hunter, not the hunted.

'How long do you plan to stay at Mannerling?' he asked abruptly.

To his horror, those beautiful eyes of hers filled with tears. 'Alas,' she said brokenly, 'I told George we had been too forward in coming. We will leave as soon as possible.'

He immediately felt like a brute. 'My dear Miss Santerton, you and your brother are welcome to be my guests for as long as you wish.'

She dabbed at her eyes. 'Too kind,' she said. 'I must do something to repay you. Your poor children, I am sure, would appreciate some feminine company. I would be prepared to spend some time with them.'

'As to that, although I do thank you for your offer, the matter is attended to. Mark and Beth go daily to Brookfield House to be educated by the governess there, an estimable woman, and they also have the company of the Beverley girls.'

'Ah, yes, the Beverleys,' she said in a low voice. 'You do not think the many scandals attached to that unfortunate family will affect your children?'

'I have heard all the scandals and no, I do not. They are very happy.'

'Mmm. Oh, well, if you are satisfied ... I mean, I trust the girls are not using the children to ingratiate themselves with you.'

'Hardly. Miss Rachel gave me my character over my neglect of Mark and Beth.'

'We shall see,' said Minerva. 'We shall see.'

*   *   *

The ball wound to its close. Rachel had not been asked to dance by Charles Blackwood and she felt it was something of a slight, for he had danced with both Lizzie and Belinda, a Belinda who, Rachel thought, had flirted quite outrageously.

She felt suddenly tired. The room was overwarm, faces were flushed, and quite a number of the gentlemen were drunk. But she knew her mother would not leave the ball until the general did. Rachel reflected that she had never seen her mother look so animated before. She still had a handsome figure and a neat ankle. She had rouged her face with two bright circles, despite Miss Trumble's advice to the contrary, in an effort to banish the pallor caused by long bouts of imaginary illness when she was mured up in her bedchamber. But Rachel noticed how the general's eyes kept straying to where Miss Trumble sat against the wall, and feared ructions ahead. Lady Beverley would have been shocked could she have guessed that the general's reasons for not taking Miss Trumble up for a dance were because he feared she might make life difficult for her governess.

At last Rachel, dancing a second dance with Mr. Cater, saw the Mannerling party leave and knew that they could now go home. Mr. Cater sought out Lady Beverley and gained her permission to call.

'He would do very well for you, Rachel,' said Lady Beverley in the carriage on the road home.

'You go too fast, Mama,' pleaded Rachel wearily. 'I know very little about the gentleman except that he owns sugar plantations in Barbados in the West Indies. He employs slaves.'

'I should be very surprised if he did not, my child. How else is the sugar to be harvested?'

But Rachel did not feel like entering into an argument on the rights and wrongs of slavery with her mother. The next day was Sunday, so there would be no visit from the Blackwood children, although they could expect to see the

Blackwoods in church.

When Rachel was brushing out her hair before going to bed, Miss Trumble quietly entered the room.

'You look worried, Rachel. Was Mr. Cater not to your liking?'

'He is a very pleasant man. But he keeps slaves. The slave-trade was abolished, or so you told us.'

'The Abolition of the Slave Trade Act was passed in 1807,' said Miss Trumble. 'But this act, be it remembered, did not abolish slavery but only prohibited the traffic in slaves. So that no ship should clear out from any port in the British dominions after May the first, 1807, with slaves on board, and that no slave should be landed in the colonies after March the first, 1808.'

'So why is there still slavery?'

Miss Trumble sat down with a weary little sigh.

'The product is now home-grown, just like the sugar. Slavery has been going on so long that there are black children growing up into slavery.'

'It distresses me,' said Rachel in a low voice.

'Many things in this wicked world distress me,' said the governess. 'But you are not going to reform a plantation owner. Should you marry him, all you could do would be to see that the slaves were well-housed and fed and not ill-treated. With the education I have given

84

you, you would be well-equipped to educate them. But in order to go to such a situation on the other side of the world, you would need to be very much in love. Arranged marriages often work out quite comfortably in England, but it would be different there. There would be so many stresses and strains.'

'It looked very much tonight as if our Mr. Charles will make a match of it with Miss Santerton.'

'I do hope not.'

'Why do you say that?'

'A feeling, that is all. I think there is an instability of mind there.'

Rachel gave a little shrug. 'Where such beauty is concerned, I am sure a little madness would not even be noticed.'

'Perhaps,' said Miss Trumble.

*　　　*　　　*

At church in the morning, with the congregation heavy-eyed after the ball the night before, Rachel noticed that the Santertons were there, Minerva and Charles looking very much a couple. Mr. Stoddart, the vicar, preached in a monotonous voice. 'I do wish that little man would end. Is he going to prose on forever?' Minerva's voice sounded in the church with dreadful clarity. Mr. Stoddart flushed, but smiled down at the Mannerling party in an ingratiating way and brought his sermon to an abrupt close.

Outside the church, where ladies clutched their bonnets in a frisky, blustery wind, Mary took hold of Rachel's arm in a confidential way. 'It looks as if Mannerling will soon have a new mistress. And so suitable!'

Rachel felt irritated and depressed at the same time. At that moment, the wind came to her rescue and whipped Mary's straw bonnet from her head and sent it scuttling off among the tombstones, with Mary in pursuit.

At least Isabella will soon be with us, thought Rachel, her eyes straying to where Charles Blackwood was escorting Minerva to the Mannerling carriage. Charles had not spoken to her or acknowledged her presence.

She did not know that Charles had had every intention of speaking, not only to her, but to various other parishioners, but that Minerva's hand on his arm had been like a vice and that, outside the church, she had instantly claimed that the sermon had given her a headache and that she wanted to return 'home.'

As his carriage drove off, he saw that new fellow, Hercules Cater, approach the Beverley family and saw a smile of welcome on Lady Beverley's thin lips.

Though he was finding Minerva a heady and enchanting beauty, she was beginning to annoy him. He did not like the unspoken and yet calm assumption of brother and sister that he should propose to Minerva.

Lady Beverley had invited Mr. Cater back to Brookfield House for a cold collation. Miss Trumble had planned to find out as much as she could about the young man, but Lady Beverley was annoyed that Charles had not spoken to her and blamed the presence of the governess. Lady Beverley always had to have someone to blame. And so she gave Miss Trumble several tasks to perform, telling her that her presence was not needed in company. Miss Trumble went in search of Barry.

'I suppose Mr. Cater will be deemed suitable for Rachel,' she said as Barry straightened up from weeding a flower-bed. 'I suppose one cannot expect all the Beverley girls to marry for love.'

'He seems a pleasant-enough young man, miss. Sugar plantations, I believe.'

'Rachel is troubled by the fact that he keeps slaves.'

'They all do, in them parts. One young miss can't change the way things are done.'

'No, but she would either need to become hardened to the situation, which I would not like, or become distressed by it. I cannot think Mr. Cater is suitable, and yet he is surely better than some elderly gentleman with a great deal of money, for I cannot see Lady Beverley balking at anyone at all who is in funds.'

'It amazes me, miss,' said Barry, 'that she is

not throwing Miss Rachel at Mr. Blackwood's head.'

'Ah, that is because my lady plans to wed the general and so secure Mannerling.'

'Any hope there?'

'I should not think so. Lady Beverley was once a very great beauty but I do not think she ever had the arts to charm. She probably relied on her beauty and fortune and felt she did not have to do much else.'

'I did hear tell that Miss Santerton is of outstanding beauty and people are already saying a match is expected.'

'Perhaps. She is certainly amazingly handsome. But tall, very tall. I always feel such a lady is to be admired from a distance, like a statue. She lacks human qualities. I have written to an old friend for the full story of the Santertons. I will let you know when her reply arrives, although it should be some days because I wrote the letter last night and cannot post it until tomorrow.'

Barry gave her a sly grin. 'It always amazes me, if I may say so, miss, that a lady like yourself would gossip with an old servant like me.'

'That is because I am an old servant myself.' Miss Trumble gathered her shawl about her shoulders, nodded to him, and walked away.

As she approached the house, she could hear a burst of laughter from the dining-room. Mr.

Cater appeared to be keeping the company well-entertained.

* * *

Only Rachel wondered at Mr. Cater's conversation. He spoke of Barbados, of the climate, of the flora and fauna, of the tedium of the long sea voyage home, of the plays he had seen in London before travelling to the country, and yet he revealed nothing of his private life, of his family, or of where he originally came from and what had taken him to the other side of the world in the first place.

But Rachel chided herself on looking for flaws. To marry such a man would mean being well set up for life, of getting away from Mama, of having a household of her own. It would be adventurous to go to the Indies.

But after the meal, when Mr. Cater asked her to show him the garden, Rachel irritated her mother by promptly suggesting that Belinda and Lizzie should accompany them. She described plants and bushes and all the while her errant thoughts kept straying to Mannerling. Had Charles considered his children if he was thinking of marriage again?

* * *

At that moment, Minerva was entering the drawing-room, holding Mark by one hand and Beth by the other. 'We have had such sport,' she cried. 'I quite dote on the children. Playing with them makes me feel like a child myself.'

'Come here to me,' said Charles to the children. 'What have you been doing?'

'Playing with stick and ball,' said Mark in a low voice. Minerva had asked them whether they did not miss their mother, and he had replied, truthfully, that he could remember very little of his mother, for he had barely seen her. Minerva had then told him that he must always put his father's happiness before any selfish thoughts, and should his father decide to find them a new mother, then he and Beth must do all in their power to make that lady welcome.

And Mark did not like Minerva. Her intense blue gaze unnerved him. But he did not want his father to retreat back into becoming the sad-eyed, withdrawn man he had been so recently and so Mark forced himself to look pleased with Minerva. He longed for Sunday to be over so that he and Beth could return to Miss Trumble and the safety of Brookfield House.

*   *   *

The Santertons slept late. On Monday morning, Charles surprised his father as he was getting into the carriage to go to Brookfield House with the children.

'Feel a bit dull,' said the general. 'Thought

I'd talk to that Trumble female. Very sensible.'

'I'll come with you,' said Charles suddenly. He did not know what it was about Mannerling that had suddenly begun to oppress him. Perhaps it was Minerva, and yet, had he been a superstitious man, he could have believed the house itself was turning against him. He could sense a malignancy lurking in its quiet rooms, but decided he was becoming fanciful and that the haunting of his son was putting him on his guard, for whoever had played such an evil trick had not been discovered.

When they arrived, Miss Trumble said that as the day was fine and warm, she would give the children their lessons in the garden. Lady Beverley urged the general and Charles to step into the house but, to her irritation, the general said he would like to sit in the garden as well.

The girls joined them. Miss Trumble started by reading items of news from the *Morning Post*, explaining before she did so that she liked the children to be au fait with current affairs. Then an article caught her eye and she began to laugh.

'What amuses you, Miss Trumble?' asked the general.

'I just read a few sentences. It appears to be a very good description of a Bond Street Lounger.'

'Read it to us,' urged the general.

'Come now, General,' protested Lady

Beverley. 'You would not like to see the education of your grandchildren neglected.'

'I think Mark should know all about Bond Street Loungers. Go ahead, Miss Trumble.'

Miss Trumble looked inquiringly at her mistress.

'Very well,' said Lady Beverley huffily.

Miss Trumble explained. 'It begins with the necessary behaviour of a Bond Street Lounger in an hotel as he tries to establish his character as that of a man of fashion. "In short, find fault with every single article without exception, damn the waiter—"'

'Miss Trumble!' exclaimed Lady Beverley.

'Go on, do,' said the general with a laugh.

'"—the waiter at almost regular intervals, and never let him stand one moment still, but keep him eternally moving; having it in remembrance that he is only an unfortunate and wretched subordinate, of course, a stranger to feelings which are an ornament to Human Nature; with this recollection on your part that the more illiberal the abuse he has from you, the greater will be his admiration of your superior abilities, and Gentleman-like qualifications. Confirm him in the opinion he has so unjustly imbibed, by swearing the fish is not warm through; the poultry is as tough as your Grandmother; the pastry is made with butter, rank Irish; the cheese which they call Stilton is nothing but pale Suffolk; the malt liquor damnable, a mere infusion of malt,

92

tobacco, and cocculus Indicus; the port musty; the sherry sour; and that the whole of the dinner and dessert were infernally infamous, and of course, not fit for the entertainment of a Gentleman; conclude the lecture with an oblique hint that, without better accommodations, and more ready attention, you shall be under the necessity of leaving the house for a more comfortable situation.

' "Having thus introduced you to, and fixed you, recruit-like, in good quarters, I consider it almost unnecessary to say, however bad you may imagine the wine, I doubt not your own prudence will point out the characteristic necessity of drinking enough, not only to afford you the credit of reeling to bed by aid of the banister, but the collateral comfort of calling yourself damned queer in the morning, owing entirely to the villainous adulteration of the wine, for when mild and genuine, you can take three bottles without winking or blinking. When rousing from your last somniferous reverie in the morning, ring the bell with no small degree of energy, which will serve to convince the whole family you are awake; upon the entrance of either chamberlain or chambermaid, vociferate half a dozen questions without waiting for a single reply. As, What morning is it? Is my breakfast ready? Has anybody inquired for me? Is my groom here? And so on and so forth. And here it becomes directly in point to observe that a groom is become so evidently necessary to the ton of the present day (particularly in the neighbourhood of Bond Street) that a great number of gentlemen keep a groom who cannot (except upon credit) keep a horse; but then, they are always on the look-out for horses, and, till they are obtained, the employment of the groom is the embellishment of his master, by first dressing his head, and then polishing his boots and shoes.'

'And I really think that is enough of that,' said Miss Trumble, putting down the paper.

'I think it is very funny,' voiced Mark.

'Prime,' said the general. 'Is there any more?'

'If there is,' said Lady Beverley, 'I pray you will restrain your language, Miss Trumble.'

'Perhaps later...'

'No, do go on,' said Rachel. 'I have seen such gentlemen when we were in London and have never heard one better described.'

Miss Trumble smiled and began to read again. '"The trifling ceremonies of the morning gone through, you will sally forth in search of adventures, taking that great Mart of every virtue, Bond Street, in your way.

'"Here it will be impossible for you (between the hours of twelve and four) to remain, even for a few minutes, without falling in with various feathers of your wing, so true it is, in the language of Rowe, you herd together, that you cannot fear being long alone. So soon as three of you are met, link your arms so as to

94

engross the whole breadth of the pavement; the fun of driving fine women and old dons into the gutter is exquisite and, of course, constitutes a laugh of the most humane sensibility. Never make these excursions without spurs, it will afford not only the presumptive proof of your really keeping a horse, but the lucky opportunity of hooking a fine girl by the gown, apron, or petticoat; and while she is under the distressing mortification of disentangling herself, you and your companions can add to her dilemma by some delicate innuendo, and, in the moment of extrication, walk off with an exulting exclamation of having *cracked the muslin*. Let it be a fixed rule never to be seen in the Lounge without a stick or cane, this, dangling on a string, may accidentally get between the feet of any female in passing; if she falls, in consequence, that can be no fault of yours, but the effect of her indiscretion.'

'Now, that really is enough, General,' said Miss Trumble. 'I am amusing you and everyone by this description, but at the moment such brutes, however satirized, are beyond the comprehension of little Beth.'

'Yes, I find your ideas of teaching most strange, Miss Trumble.' Having delivered herself of that reproof, Lady Beverley smiled at the general and went on, 'And how go the Santertons?'

'Abed, I should think,' said the general gruffly. Mark and Beth had been summoned by Miss Trumble to sit at a table next to her under the shade of the cedar tree, Beth to write the letters of the alphabet in block letters and then script, and Mark to study his Latin declensions.

'I regret I did not have the chance to dance with you on Saturday night,' Charles said to Rachel. 'But every time I was free to approach you, I found you surrounded by courtiers. I believe your sister, Lady Fitzgerald, is soon to be in residence at Perival.'

Rachel's eyes lit up. 'Oh, I am so looking forward to seeing her again. And her children. They are too young, alas, to be companions for Mark. The boy needs children of his own age.'

'And what would you suggest I do to remedy that?'

Rachel laughed. 'You will begin to think I am always advising you as to what to do with your children when it is none of my affair.'

'I would appreciate such advice.'

'You could give a children's party for Mark. Miss Trumble could furnish you with a list of suitable children in the neighbourhood.'

'It is his birthday in a week's time. Perhaps that is too soon?'

'I am sure Miss Trumble will be able to arrange something.'

The general had risen to his feet and was heading in the direction of where Miss Trumble sat with Mark and Beth.

'Come now, General.' Lady Beverley's voice

called him back. 'I am become stiff with sitting here. Let us take a promenade together.'

The general returned to her side, throwing an anguished look in the direction of his son which went unnoticed by Charles, for Rachel was talking about Mr. Cater and Charles asked her, rather sharply, if she really knew anything at all about the man.

'As to that,' said Rachel, 'I know very little other than what he tells us about himself, that he is a sugar planter from Barbados and is here in England on quite a long visit.'

'No doubt to find himself a wife.'

'Perhaps. And yet Mannerling appears to be his goal.'

'In what way?'

'He heard it described to him by an old friend of my father's and in such glowing terms that he decided to travel here and see the place for himself.'

'Strange.'

'How strange?'

'Mostly gentlemen such as Mr. Cater come armed with letters of introduction.'

'Perhaps he could not find anyone who knows you.'

'I have a large acquaintance in London and I believe he spent some time there.'

'It could be that he does not move in the same circles as you do yourself, sir.'

'Any sugar planter who appears to be as rich as Mr. Cater, to judge from his clothes and carriage, would most certainly move in fashionable circles.'

Some imp prompted Rachel to say, 'Perhaps I will wed Mr. Cater and travel to the West Indies.'

'I was not aware that you were so enchanted with him.'

'If you have visited Lady Evans and also remember my sister Lizzie's ill-timed and ill-judged remarks, you will know that I do not command much in the way of a dowry and so must take the best bidder.'

His face darkened and his eyes glittered like green ice. 'Does none of your sex ever marry out of affection?'

She quailed before his gaze and said, 'Yes, my three sisters, the ones who are already wed. Do not look so furiously at me, I pray. I was funning. I know little of Mr. Cater and have no ambitions in that direction.'

But he still looked angry as his eyes went past her to where a carriage was turning into the short drive. Rachel swung round in time to see Minerva being helped down from the carriage by her brother. Minerva was wearing a muslin gown which clung to her form like the folds of drapery on a statue. Her hair was in a plait at the back, and falling in small ringlets around her face and shining with *huile antique*. On top of her head was a small round hat embellished on the front with three scarlet feathers which had been moulded to look like burning flames. She carried a parasol of white lace.

George Santerton was wearing a long-tailed blue coat with gold buttons, a high starched cravat, and shirt-points so high that they dug into his cheeks. His waistcoat was canary yellow and hung with fobs and seals. He had lavender gloves and lavender shoes on his small feet. Rachel wondered if such a tall man could really have such small feet. Large feet were considered a social disgrace, as was a large mouth, and so many men thrust their tortured feet into shoes several sizes too small for them.

The two fashion plates, brother and sister, had probably planned to make an entrance, but once they had arrived and were settled in chairs in the garden, the sheer formality of their attire seemed out of place.

And Rachel became conscious that Minerva's blue gaze was often fixed on her in an assessing, calculating way. It could not be that Minerva regarded her as a rival! But Rachel began to think that was the case and it made her look at Charles Blackwood in a different light. For the first time, she really saw him as an attractive man, not just handsome and wealthy, but a man to be desired.

A flush mounted to her cheeks. Charles looked quickly at her and she dropped her eyes and twisted a handkerchief in her lap.

And Minerva looked at both of them.

CHAPTER FOUR

At ev'ry word a reputation dies.

ALEXANDER POPE

A week later and Miss Trumble had gone to supervise the fairly impromptu party to be held for Mark at Mannerling and Rachel was being taken out on a drive by Mr. Cater. Her new sharp awareness of Charles Blackwood had made her completely indifferent to Mr. Cater's company and she was annoyed that this drive had been organized by her mother, without consulting her first.

Mr. Cater had been to Mannerling and was rhapsodizing about it. For the first time, Rachel found all these descriptions and eulogies of her former home tedious in the extreme. She interrupted a description of the glory of the painted ceilings by asking abruptly, 'Where is your family from, Mr. Cater?'

'We are from Suffolk.'

'Indeed. And when did you go to Barbados?'

'Five years ago.'

'With your parents?'

'No, Miss Rachel. My uncle bought me a passage. My parents died when I was a child.'

'And did this uncle own the sugar

100

plantation?'

'No, he did not.'

'So how...?'

'Miss Rachel, I am here in England on this beautiful sunny day with a beautiful companion. For the moment, I wish to forget about the Indies.'

'I am sorry if my curiosity offends you, sir.'

'I miss England,' he said. 'I miss the greenery. I miss the life. I am not comfortable in Barbados.'

'But I was under the impression that...'

'I loved the place? It is where I work. I am thinking of selling up.'

'And where would you live? Suffolk?'

'There is nothing for me there. Mannerling appears to have a sad history. You knew the subsequent owners, of course.'

'Yes, there was a Mr. Judd. The poor man committed suicide. Then there was the Devers family. Such a scandal. You have surely heard all about it. The son, Harry, was killed falling from a roof in London, trying to escape the law. He was obsessed with Mannerling, as was Mr. Judd.'

He shot her a sly look. 'As are the Beverleys, or so I was led to believe.'

'You *have* been listening to the local gossip,' said Rachel with a lightness she did not feel. 'Yes, in our case, the loss of our home hit us very hard. But we are become accustomed to our new life. The Blackwoods are very good owners, very suitable.'

'And you no longer desire the place?'

'I do not desire what is not possible to have.'

'Everything is possible. Even Mannerling.'

Rachel fell silent. Just suppose she wished to marry Charles. How impossible that would be! He, too, knew the tales about the Beverleys' plotting and scheming to get their old home back and would look on any overtures from her with deep suspicion. She wished somehow that she could still regard him as a much older person, not marriageable, but his face rose in her mind's eye, strong and handsome with those odd green eyes, and she was only dimly aware that Mr. Cater was still talking of Mannerling.

*   *   *

There were eight children at Mark's party, all having a marvellous time playing games organized by Miss Trumble. The Long Gallery was being used for the party and a table with cakes and jellies and jugs of lemonade had been set up at the end of the gallery.

All went well until Minerva made her entrance, carrying a book. 'I am sure you are in need of some rest,' she said to Miss Trumble. 'I have told the housekeeper to prepare you something in the servants' hall.'

'Thank you,' said Miss Trumble. 'But I am not hungry.'

'Oh, I am sure you are. Please do as you are told.'

Miss Trumble curtsied. The children, left alone with the statuesque Minerva, looked at her wide-eyed.

Minerva pulled forward a chair and sat down and opened her book. 'Gather round me in a circle,' she ordered. She planned to begin reading to them and then ring for a servant to summon Charles so that he could see how well she got on with children.

They sat round her in a circle at her feet. She had found a book of children's stories in the library and she began to read about a little boy who had lost his mother and behaved badly to his father. As she read, she kept flashing meaningful little looks at Mark.

Mark felt his temper rising. It was *his* party and Minerva was not only ruining it but telling that stupid story about some stupid boy who was nasty to his widowed father. Minerva paused and rang the bell and told a footman to fetch Mr. Blackwood and then continued to read.

With the perspicacity of the very young, Mark guessed what she was about. His father should not see the pretty picture she made reading to the children. He rose to his feet.

'Where are you going, Mark?' demanded Minerva sharply.

'I am going to get something to eat,' said Mark haughtily.

The other children rose as well.

'Come back here!' ordered Minerva.

'Do not pay her any heed,' commanded Mark. 'She don't live here. Come along.'

Mischievously delighted at the idea of disobeying authority, the children followed Mark to the table and began to spoon jelly onto plates.

Minerva's temper flared. She marched up to the table and seized Beth, who was the nearest child, in a strong grip. 'You will all return to the reading!'

'Leave her alone!' shouted Mark, turning red in the face.

Beth gave a whimper of fright. Mark seized a plate containing a large green jelly and flung it straight into Minerva's face just as the door opened and his father walked in, followed by Miss Trumble.

'You little whoreson!' screamed Minerva, clawing green jelly from her face.

'What is going on here?' thundered Charles.

Beth, finding herself released, ran to Miss Trumble and buried her face in that lady's skirts.

Minerva began to cry.

Mark stood, white-faced at the enormity of what he had just done.

'I w-was m-merely trying to entertain the ch-children,' sobbed Minerva, 'when Mark threw jelly all over me.'

'Miss Trumble, take the children to another

room,' ordered Charles. 'Not you, Mark.' He turned to John, the footman, who had entered and was avidly watching the scene. 'You, escort Miss Santerton to her quarters and fetch her lady's-maid.'

Miss Trumble took both children and book with her. Minerva left with the footman. Mark and his father faced each other.

'Well?' demanded Charles. 'I am waiting.'

Mark hung his head.

'Am I to understand that Miss Terry perhaps had the right of it and that you need to be beaten?'

Mark could not find any words.

The door opened again and Miss Trumble came in, carrying the book from which Minerva had been reading.

Charles swung round angrily. 'I think you should leave this to me and attend to your duties, Miss Trumble.'

'If you will bear with me, sir,' said Miss Trumble, 'I think I can explain Mark's behaviour.'

'That is for the boy to explain. He has a tongue in his head.'

'I think he might find this difficult to put into words. Miss Santerton was reading this story to the children, which I consider most unsuitable and it is probably what upset Mark.'

'Go on.'

'It is a story about a boy who had lost his

mother and who subsequently behaved badly towards his father. It is a story I never read to children myself, or in fact anything by this author.'

'But how should this affect Mark? The boy has never behaved badly until now!'

Miss Trumble's presence and kind, understanding eyes had given Mark courage. He ran to her and clutched her hand.

'Did it upset you, Mark?' asked Miss Trumble. 'You have behaved very badly and must apologize to Miss Santerton. But we would like to hear the truth.'

'It was the way she was reading it,' said Mark. 'She kept flashing meaningful little looks at me and Miss Santerton had already said something to me about having a new mother and I knew she wanted my father to think she could fulfil that role, and I am ... frightened of her.'

'Let me see that story,' ordered Charles.

Miss Trumble handed him the book. He studied it in silence while Mark gripped Miss Trumble's hand even harder.

Charles felt his fury abating. He had never, he realized, stopped to consider what the loss of their mother had meant to Mark. He had been wrapped in his own fury at her infidelity and then his shock at her sudden death. The boy could not be allowed to get away with such behaviour, but he could not bring himself to beat him, or order a beating.

He could not believe that Minerva had been so crude as to hint that she might be the children's new mother. He looked helplessly at Miss Trumble.

'I suggest you leave matters to me, sir,' she said quietly. 'The children are guests and are not to be collected for another hour. I suggest the party should go on. After the party is over, Mark will apologize most humbly to Miss Santerton and I can take things from there.'

'I am so sorry,' whispered Mark.

'Run along, Mark. You will find Beth and your new friends in the drawing-room.'

When the boy had left, Miss Trumble said, 'May I ask, sir, whether Mark loved his mother very much?'

Charles sighed and put the book carefully down on a console table. 'I do not think he saw much of her except for a few glimpses. He was passed to a wet-nurse immediately he was born and then to the nursemaid and then to Miss Terry. But he has grossly insulted a guest in my house and that must not be allowed to go unpunished.'

'No, I will see to that.'

Miss Trumble curtsied and went to join the party and found the drawing-room quiet and silent. The little group of scared children sat around Mark.

She clapped her hands briskly. 'This will not do. Did I tell you about the treasure hunt?'

'No!' they all chorused.

'I will hand you all slips of paper with your first clue. The treasure is hidden somewhere in the house. I suggest you hunt in pairs. Mark, you go with your little sister.' Miss Trumble paired off the rest. Soon the children were off hunting through the great house.

'Where do you think the treasure is?' Beth asked Mark.

'I really don't care,' he said. 'All I can think of is that I have got to apologize to Miss Santerton. I am in deep disgrace.'

Beth suddenly giggled. 'She did look such a guy with green jelly all over her.'

Mark hugged her. 'It would be almost worth it if Father were not so upset.'

'Will he marry her? Will she be our new mother? I should not like that.'

'It is something we may have to face. Drat! If only I could get this horrible apology over and done with.'

'We could go now,' suggested Beth eagerly. 'S'pose so.'

Hand in hand, they walked to the west wing and stopped outside Minerva's door.

Mark reached for the door handle and then stopped.

'What is it?' hissed Beth.

'There is someone in there with her. Shh!'

Mark leaned his ear against the door panels.

'Someone's coming out,' he said. He seized Beth's hand. There was a window in the passage opposite the door. He pulled Beth into the embrasure and drew the curtains closed.

He heard the door of Minerva's room open and her brother George's voice sounded clearly, ''Pon rep, sis, you are become over-exercised about a pair of spoilt brats. Marry Blackwood, send the boy packing to school, give the girl a strict governess, and then you need never have anything to do with them again.'

'You forget'—Minerva's voice—'he seems too interested in them to turn a blind eye to their affairs.'

'You know how to make men love you, do you not? Get him in your wiles and the man will forget he even has children.'

'I would like to get rid of that Trumble creature. I have an enemy there.'

'Pooh, what can a faded old spinster like that do?'

'More than you think. Have you noticed the way the general eyes her? If I do not play my cards right, then that old governess will be mistress at Mannerling and I will not!'

'What are you going to do? Kill her?' George gave a great braying laugh.

'Oh, go away,' snapped his sister, 'and leave me to prepare for the great apology scene which is no doubt soon to take place.'

The children waited, hearing George's footsteps die away along the long corridor and then all was silent.

They finally crept out. 'Not now,' whispered

Mark. 'I could not face her now.'

*　　　*　　　*

'I heard from the housekeeper at Mannerling that the place is haunted,' Mr. Cater was saying to Rachel.

'It is not haunted. Someone tried to frighten the little boy by dressing up as the ghost of the late Mr. Judd.'

'Are you sure it was not a ghost?'

'Our servant, Barry, managed to strike the ghost on the head. His cudgel contacted a human head and not a ghostly one.'

'You are unromantic, Miss Rachel. I, for one, am prepared to believe that Mannerling is haunted.'

Rachel gave a laugh. 'In all the time I lived there, I never saw even one ghost. There is nothing at Mannerling to frighten anyone.'

*　　　*　　　*

The party finished with Gerrard, a local farmer's boy, finding the treasure, which turned out to be a toy sword and a box of paints. The other children all received consolation prizes and went off happily in various gigs and carriages.

Mark was taken by his father to Minerva's apartment in the west wing, where he apologized most humbly. To his surprise, and

110

then his dismay, instead of railing at him, Minerva drew him to her and hugged him and said, 'I should have known such a story would upset a poor motherless child like you. There. We have both apologized and now we can be friends.'

She smiled down at him and Mark felt himself trapped in that intense blue gaze. His father was looking at Minerva with a softened look on his normally harsh face.

Mark repeated again in a dull, flat little voice that he was very, very sorry and then turned to his father and asked if he could leave. 'Off with you,' said his father, 'and consider yourself a lucky young man. Few ladies would have accepted an apology for such rank behaviour with such grace and charity as Miss Santerton.'

*   *   *

When the Santertons and the Blackwoods had retired to their rooms to dress for dinner, Miss Trumble made her way through the suddenly quiet house to go down to the hall and wait for the carriage to be brought round to take her home.

She paused at the top of the staircase, listening to the quiet of the house. And then she realized it was not really quiet. There had always been many clocks at Mannerling and the general, who collected them, had added a great deal more.

111

She became aware of the restless ticking and tocking, which seemed to be getting louder as if innumerable little voices were whispering away the time. 'Hurry, hurry, hurry,' went the voices. 'You are old, old, old, and time is running out for you.'

She walked stiffly down the stairs, hearing all those time voices chattering away, feeling a sort of brooding menace emanating from the walls. She gave herself a mental shake. Mannerling was a large house, nothing more. It was unlike her to let her fancies get the better of her.

And then, as she reached the hall, the grandfather clock against the far wall boomed out five hours and from all over the house came the clamour of chimes, until all the tinkling and booming and chiming seemed to merge together in one great mocking, triumphant sound.

Miss Trumble wrenched open the great front door and went out into the sunlight and took a deep breath. The carriage swept up to the front of the house and a footman ran out and let down the steps. Miss Trumble climbed in, feeling shaken.

She felt suddenly that Mannerling was no place for those little children. Perhaps the menace she had felt came from Minerva's presence.

Her fancies apart, someone had tried to frighten Mark. What kind of person would

112

play such a trick on a child?

Perhaps when the eldest sister, Isabella, arrived, she could arrange for the children to spend much of their time between Brookfield House and Perival, away from the menace of Mannerling.

*   *   *

Sanity, like a breath of fresh air, blew into Miss Trumble's worried life with the arrival of Isabella, Lady Fitzpatrick, her husband, and his aunt, Mrs. Kennedy.

At first Miss Trumble thought Isabella might be a trifle haughty, but then Isabella had taken her aside and asked anxiously, 'And how goes Barry?'

'Do you mean our odd man? Very well, and a comfort to us all.'

'He was a very great comfort to me with his kindness and good sense.'

'Would you like to see him? We could take a turn in the garden.'

'I would like that above all things.'

When they were outside, Miss Trumble received another surprise, for the tall and elegant Isabella linked her arm in that of the governess in a companionable way and said, 'Barry writes to me from time to time. I hear great things of you.'

Miss Trumble actually found herself blushing for the first time in years. 'That is very gratifying.'

Barry walked across the back lawn to greet them, his cap in his hand, a broad smile on his face.

'Well, well, well, my lady, you do be a sight for sore eyes.'

'Does all go well, Barry?'

'Very well, my lady. Are the children with you?'

'They are with their nurse, but you shall visit us and see them for yourself. I do not want to deprive the excellent Miss Trumble or my sisters of your help, Barry, but I do wish you would return with us to Ireland.'

'Maybe soon, Miss Isabella, I mean, my lady.'

'You may call me Miss Isabella if you wish.'

If only my three girls could turn out like this eldest sister, thought Miss Trumble. If only they, too, could escape Mannerling.

'So I believe there is a new owner at Mannerling,' said Isabella, 'but fortunately of an age too old to tempt my sisters.'

'As to that,' said Barry cautiously, 'he do be a remarkably handsome man and don't look a bit his age.'

'Aha!' Isabella looked quizzically at Miss Trumble. 'And when I asked Rachel why she had not gone to London for a Season, she hummed and hawed and then said it was because of my impending visit.'

'Perhaps that was indeed the case,' said Miss

Trumble evasively.

'And Mama seems in alt over the father, General Blackwood. Never say she has hopes in that direction.'

'That is not for me to say,' said Miss Trumble primly. 'But the carriage from Mannerling will be here shortly to collect the children and I must not be found neglecting my duties in case Mr. Blackwood comes himself. Mark has extra lessons as a punishment for an impertinence.'

She curtsied and left.

'Miss Trumble is as you described her to be,' said Isabella to Barry. 'But I was not prepared to find such a grand lady. Her style and clothes are modish. Where did she come from?'

'Ah, that's a mystery,' said Barry. 'I believe she gave Lady Beverley references at last.'

'Perhaps she is of good family and fallen on hard times.'

'Now that's the puzzle, my lady, for to tell the truth, Lady Beverley often does not pay her and yet she always seems to be in funds.'

'Strange. I shall leave you now, Barry and we will talk again. I hear the carriage arriving for the children and I am anxious to see this new owner should he be there.'

When Isabella rounded the corner of the house, she stopped short. A tall man was alighting from a curricle. He looked at her curiously and then bowed and smiled. Why, he is almost as handsome as my husband, marvelled Isabella, who never thought any man in the world could match Lord Fitzpatrick.

'Lady Fitzpatrick,' he said with a bow.

'You must be Mr. Blackwood.' Isabella curtsied. 'You are come for your children. But you must meet my husband and Mrs. Kennedy before you leave.'

They walked into the house together. The company was gathered in the little-used drawing-room.

Charles was introduced all round.

Isabella covertly watched Rachel. It was as if every fibre of her younger sister's body was aware of this Mr. Blackwood. And yet he treated her with the same easy manner as he treated Lizzie and Belinda.

Despite his age, thought Isabella, he should be very aware of such a beautiful girl as Rachel. No man could look at her and remain indifferent.

And then the maid, Betty, came in and announced, 'Miss Santerton.'

Isabella's eyes swung to the doorway and she blinked at the vision that stood there. She did not notice the flash of irritation in Charles's eyes. All Isabella could think was, poor Rachel. This is too much competition.

Minerva was wearing a wide straw hat decorated with a whole garden of flowers. Her muslin gown was so fine it was nearly transparent and floated around her excellent

116

body as she moved. The underdress was very fitting and was of pale-pink silk, which gave the impression that she had nothing on underneath. Her eyes caressed Charles in an intimate way.

She greeted Isabella and her husband effusively but looked down on the dumpy figure of Mrs. Kennedy and offered her two fingers to shake. Mrs. Kennedy flashed the beauty a look of contempt and sat down, ignoring those two fingers.

Charles had taken a liking to the broad-spoken, warm-hearted little Irishwoman who was Mrs. Kennedy and felt suddenly ashamed of Minerva. Here were the despised Beverleys, supposed to be grasping and ambitious, and yet they seemed kind and gentle to him. He had warmed towards Minerva since—what he considered—her gracious acceptance of Mark's apology, but now he began to wish she and her brother would leave. George was a tiresome bore who drank too much at dinner and then said the same thing over and over again.

Minerva was clever enough to realize her social gaffe had annoyed Charles and so she sat down next to Mrs. Kennedy and asked, 'Did you have an arduous journey?'

'Sure, me dears,' said Mrs. Kennedy, getting to her feet and waddling towards the door. 'I think we had best be getting off. Do come and see us as soon as possible.'

'Tomorrow,' cried Lizzie.

'Faith, tomorrow, tonight, any time you like, my chuck.'

Minerva smiled. 'My brother and I are resident at Mannerling, Mrs. Kennedy. We would be pleased to call on you.'

Before Isabella could reply, Mrs. Kennedy said roundly, 'That will not be convenient. We are all still mighty fatigued after our journey and wish to see only the family. Good day to you.'

'Dreadful woman!' complained Minerva to Charles on the road back to Mannerling.

'Mrs. Kennedy? I found her excellent. She took you in dislike, as any of lady of her standing would, at being offered only two fingers to shake. You brought that snub on yourself.'

'But how was I to know? Such a fat little creature and that quiz of a bonnet! I thought she was the maid.'

'Fitzpatrick said very clearly that she was his aunt.'

They continued the journey in silence, a silence which enlivened Mark's spirits. He could feel the threat of his father's ever marrying Minerva receding.

*   *   *

At one o'clock the following morning, Miss Trumble was roused by one of the maids who

118

gasped out, 'You are to dress and go to Mannerling. A carriage is arrived.'

She handed Miss Trumble a letter. Miss Trumble got out of bed and took the candle from the maid and read it. It was from Charles Blackwood. The 'haunting' of Mannerling had started again and the children were frightened out of their wits.

'I shall help you dress, miss,' said the maid, Betty.

'No, rouse Miss Rachel and help her dress instead. Tell her I wish her to come with me.'

It was a windy night, with a small moon running through the ragged clouds overhead as the great bulk of Mannerling reared up. 'It must have been really bad for Mr. Blackwood to summon you in the middle of the night,' said Rachel.

'Yes, I believe someone is out to frighten those children out of their wits,' said the governess, 'and yet...'

'What were you about to say?'

'Nothing.' Miss Trumble had been about to say that at times she thought Mannerling really was haunted by some presence but she did not want to frighten Rachel.

Charles Blackwood had been looking out for their arrival and met them in the hall and led the way up the stairs.

'I am grateful to you for coming. I will take you to the children directly. Beth is in Mark's room.' He showed no surprise at Rachel's presence.

'What happened?' asked Miss Trumble.

'Sounds and moans and clanking of chains. One footman screeching he had seen a spectral figure in the Long Gallery. Ghostly voices sounding all over the house.'

'Was that footman John?'

'No, Henry, the other second footman.'

The children were lying huddled together in Mark's bed.

'I shall go back through the house with Mr. Blackwood,' said Miss Trumble firmly. 'Rachel and I have brought our night-clothes. Rachel, I suggest, as Mark's bed is large enough, that you get into bed with the children and read them a story until they fall asleep.'

As if seeing her for the first time, Charles said, 'This is most kind of you, Miss Rachel. I did not mean...'

'I do not mind,' said Rachel quietly.

When Charles and Miss Trumble had left, Rachel said to the scared children, 'Well, this is quite an adventure, is it not?'

'We heard the ghosts,' whispered Mark, 'shrieking and wailing.'

'What you heard,' said Rachel firmly, 'was some monster playing a trick on you. When Barry hit that man on the head, the one who was pretending to be a ghost, his cudgel struck a real head. I am going into the powder-closet to change and then I will read to you. You may have all the candles in the room burning tonight.'

She changed quickly into a night-gown, wrapper, and night-cap, and then climbed into bed between the two children, after having picked a book from the shelves along the wall. She selected a mild fairy story after a search, wondering why children's stories were so bloodthirsty.

They snuggled up to her as she began to read, and after only a few pages she realized they had both fallen asleep.

She lay for some time thinking about Charles Blackwood, thinking how strong and handsome he had looked in his silk dressing-gown and with his hair tousled. She wondered how those green eyes would look were they to shine with love. And then she drifted off to sleep as well, a smile on her lips and one arm around each child.

After Rachel had been asleep for an hour, the door opened quietly and Charles and Miss Trumble looked in.

Rachel's fair hair under her lacy night-cap was spread out on the pillow. The children were cuddled up to her on either side.

Charles gently closed the door again. 'I am most grateful to Miss Rachel,' he said to Miss Trumble.

'Rachel genuinely likes your children,' said Miss Trumble. 'They will feel safe with her and it is very important for little children to feel safe and secure.'

121

'Yes,' he said slowly, thinking of the beautiful Rachel, her face soft and vulnerable in the candle-light. 'Yes, I can see that.'

'So we have interviewed the servants and they are all badly frightened,' said Miss Trumble, 'and it seems we cannot convince them someone is fooling them.' They walked to the drawing-room, where a fire was burning brightly. 'What do Miss Santerton and her brother think of the hauntings? And your father?'

'They appear to have slept through the whole commotion and I saw no reason to rouse them.'

Miss Trumble sat down wearily. 'You must now go to bed,' he said gently. 'I am most grateful to you. I will gladly remunerate you for your efforts on my behalf.'

The governess looked at him haughtily. 'There are some things,' she said frostily, 'that you do not pay for or offer to pay for, sir.'

'My apologies,' he said, half-amused, half-exasperated by this elderly governess who could so easily put him in his place.

After a silence he said, 'If we cannot find the culprit or culprits, then what are we to do?'

'I think the best thing would be to arm some of the staff, the ones you feel you can trust, a few of the grooms as well, and post them throughout the house. Give them instructions to shoot any "ghost" on sight and tell this to the rest of your servants. Is there anyone from your past who would wish to harm you or the children, Mr. Blackwood?'

'Not that I know of.'

'Strange. And yet there is something about Mannerling that appears to create a madness in certain people.'

'Like the Beverleys?'

'They are no longer concerned with the place,' said Miss Trumble firmly. 'I was thinking of Judd and Harry Devers. Is there anyone you know who might want to drive you out of here and get Mannerling for themselves?'

'No one at all.'

'What of the Santertons? What do you know of them?'

'Not very much. I knew them in the past and they claimed such friendship with me that I was inclined to believe it. No man is immune to hearing a very beautiful woman claim friendship. But they were not responsible for the hauntings, for I looked in on both brother and sister and they were heavily asleep. Miss Santerton takes laudanum, I believe, and George had three bottles of wine at dinner.'

'In any case, do tell the staff that any apparition will be shot.'

'I will do that tomorrow, or today, rather. Do go to bed, Miss Trumble. You must be exhausted. I hope your employer will not be too angry with me for having taken you away in the middle of the night.'

'Lady Beverley will be pleased that I am able to be of help,' said Miss Trumble, privately thinking that Lady Beverley would be delighted and would probably call at Mannerling as soon as she could.

*   *   *

Minerva was getting dressed by her maid the following morning when she heard the sound of laughter from below her window. She went and opened the window and leaned out. Rachel was running across the lawn with the children. At a little distance behind them, Charles Blackwood was following them. Her face darkened and she slammed the window shut and swung round to face her lady's-maid. 'What is that Beverley creature doing at Mannerling?'

'It was the hauntings, miss.'

'What are you babbling about?'

'There were ghosts haunting the place during the night and frightening the children. Mr. Blackwood sent for that governess, Miss Trumble, to quieten the children, and she brought Miss Rachel Beverley with her.'

'So that's her game,' muttered Minerva. 'We'll see about that. Don't just stand there. Hurry and fix my hair and then fetch my brother here directly.'

When George Santerton trailed in, his sister surveyed him furiously. He was in his undress,

124

a gold silk banyan and a gold silk turban and Turkish slippers with turned-up toes. His eyes were bloodshot and he looked groggily about him.

'What's to do?'

She told him succinctly of the happenings of the night, which had resulted in that 'scheming' governess's moving her chess-piece into play, namely Rachel Beverley.

George stifled a yawn. 'That old governess don't need to scheme for her charges, if you ask me. The general's potty about her. My guess is the old boy will propose marriage.'

'A man of his standing cannot marry a governess. I thought he might propose but I realized that such an alliance would be out of the question. Don't be silly.'

'When a man gets to his age, he's apt to please himself and damn society, if you ask me. And if this place is really haunted, I'm off. Spirits frighten me.'

'Really, brother, dear? From the amount of white brandy you are capable of pouring down your useless throat, I would have thought *spirits* were the last thing to frighten you.'

'Ha ha, very funny. But don't you think it deuced odd, all these ghosts?'

'No, I don't. I think when people are dead, they stay dead.'

'Comforting thought in your case, sis.'

They eyed each other for a moment and then Minerva shrugged. 'You don't believe all that rubbish that I killed Santerton?'

'Never said I did.'

'So, to return to the main point, what do I do about Rachel Beverley?'

He sat down and buried his head in his hands, knocking his turban off onto the floor.

'Oh, why am I asking you?' Minerva paced angrily up and down. 'You're a fool.'

'So everyone keeps telling me,' said George, raising his head. 'But I tell you what, I heard gossip about those Beverleys at that country dance. Damned ambitious lot and not a feather to fly with. I think mayhap Charles needs a gentle reminder that any Beverley interested in him or his children or both is only scheming to get Mannerling back. Your trouble, sis, is that you don't like children. Come to think of it, you don't like anybody.'

'That is not true. I dote on Charles.'

'My head aches. Go off and dote on your own.' George rose abruptly and left the room.

Minerva heard the sound of carriage wheels on the drive. She looked out again.

This is all I need, she thought, as she saw the squat bulk of Mrs. Kennedy descending from the carriage.

*   *   *

Mrs. Kennedy had been told of the hauntings by the servants at Perival, who had heard the news from a maid who was being courted by one of the Mannerling grooms. She was ushered into the drawing-room by Henry, the footman, who said he would let Mr. Blackwood know she had arrived.

'Stay,' commanded Mrs. Kennedy as the footman was about to bow his way out. 'What's this about ghosts?'

The footman turned pale. 'I saw one with my own eyes, madam, at the end of the Long Gallery, a great black figure.'

'See the face?'

'No, madam, I screamed and ran away, I was so frit. And then the voices came, all over the house, wailing and shrieking.'

'Where were these voices coming from?'

'In the air, madam. From nowheres in particular.'

'Thank you. You may go.'

When the footman had left, Mrs. Kennedy sat thinking furiously. She remembered when she had been a young girl in Ireland, frightening a house party out of their wits with some of their friends. They had climbed up to the roof and had wailed and shrieked down the chimneys. She wondered if anyone had been up on the roof.

Not used to sitting still for very long, she began to fidget and then she rose to her feet and went out and up the stairs to the top of the house until she found a narrow little staircase that led up to a door which gave out onto the leads.

127

Moving nimbly on her feet, surprisingly so in such a heavily built woman, she began to search, clambering around the forest of chimneys on the roof of Mannerling. And then something bright at the edge of the roof lying in a bay formed by a little curved balustrade caught her attention. She walked into the bay and picked it up. It was a livery button, a silver button with the Blackwood crest of an oak tree on it. Her eyes gleamed as brightly as the button. Here was proof. Find the servant with a missing button and then ask the fellow what he had been doing on the roof where no one but a builder or repairman had reason to be. And then an arm went around her neck and a voice grated in her ear, 'Give that to me.'

She went very still. 'No,' she said. Her plump hand closed even more firmly around the button. The arm tightened around her neck. She could feel her heart thumping. She kicked her assailant in the shins. Her one main thought was to get herself away from the edge of the balustrade.

Despite her age, she was strong and she was powerful and she was used to danger, having followed her late husband on many army campaigns. She fought and struggled until she had swung round, facing into the house, and her attacker now had his back to the balustrade. One of her hands seized a hat-pin from her bonnet and she drove it into that arm. There was a yell of pain, she felt herself released and she drove back with both elbows with all her might into the figure behind her.

There was a tremendous scream, a scream that descended, a scream abruptly cut off.

Mrs. Kennedy sat down suddenly and began to cry.

CHAPTER FIVE

I seem to move among a world of ghosts,
And feel myself the shadow of a dream.

ALFRED, LORD TENNYSON

Minerva went out of the front door of Mannerling, her eyes narrowing as she saw Rachel, Charles, and the children approaching her across the lawns, looking like a family party.

She pinned a smile on her face. She would need to appear all that was amiable, she would need to pretend to like Rachel, and then she would try to pour some poison into Charles's ears about the plots of the Beverleys. Minerva was wearing a white lace morning gown and another wide-brimmed bonnet. Her white kid gloves were wrinkled in the current fashion and elbow-length. Her white kid shoes peeped out from under her gown. Her hat was of white straw and embellished with white silk flowers.

Minerva considered that she now looked the very picture of a virgin.

She floated towards Charles, her hands outstretched in welcome.

And then Charles shouted, 'Look out!' He ran towards her and pulled her roughly to one side as a long scream descended from the heavens towards her.

There was a sickening thump behind her. Rachel shouted to the children, 'Don't look,' and pressed their faces against her skirts.

Over their heads, she saw Charles stoop over the crumpled body which had fallen from the roof.

'Get the children inside,' shouted Charles. 'Now!'

Rachel hurried off with Mark and Beth.

'Who is it?' asked Minerva, 'And how did he come to fall?'

In all his fright and distress, part of his mind still registered how calmly Minerva appeared to be reacting to the whole thing.

'It is one of my footmen, John.'

'Oh, a *footman*!' said Minerva, and turned away as Miss Trumble came out of the house.

'It is only a footman,' said Minerva, 'fallen from the roof.'

Servants came running out of the house and over from the stables.

'Take the body inside,' ordered Charles. 'Miss Trumble, see to Rachel and the children.'

'I came to tell you Mrs. Kennedy called, but

130

I cannot find her.'

He gave an exclamation and strode ahead of the governess into the house.

A weak voice from the landing sounded down to them, Mrs. Kennedy's voice.

'I killed him,' she said. 'I couldn't help it.'

*   *   *

They were finally all gathered in the drawing-room to hear Mrs. Kennedy's amazing story. The general slowed up the telling of it by demanding to hear all about the haunting first and asking why no one had thought to rouse him.

'The question now is,' said Miss Trumble quietly, 'who employed him to do such a thing? And why did the housekeeper and that boy lie about him being present with the other servants when we were looking for the ghost of Judd?'

They were then interrupted by the arrival of Lady Beverley, and all the explanations had to be gone through again.

'Well, really,' bridled Lady Beverley, glaring at Miss Trumble, 'I should have been roused. I am the one most qualified to deal with nervous children.'

'You went to bed complaining of illness,' said Miss Trumble, 'and demanded not to be roused before noon, no matter what happened.'

'Miss Trumble and your daughter were a tower of strength,' put in Charles, but all that did was make Lady Beverley angrier than ever.

Charles rang the bell and asked for the housekeeper and the boy, Freddy, to be sent in.

Mrs. Jones came in after quite a long wait, dabbing at her eyes. 'My apologies, sir,' she said in her hoarse voice. 'I am so overset by the death of poor John.'

Barry entered the room and bowed low. 'I have some news,' he said to Charles.

'Go on.'

'I took the liberty of examining the dead fellow's head. There was a bump on it which I do not think was caused by the fall, for he fell on his left side and the blow I struck him—for I now know it must have been John—was on the right. The bump must have come up after you examined him, sir. Also in his quarters, I found this.' Barry held up a sandy wig.

Charles turned again to Mrs. Jones. 'So what have you to say for yourself? You said he was standing beside you in the hall.'

'It was afterwards that John talked to me about me standing next to him and reminded me of what he had said.'

'But you must have remembered yourself whether he was there or not!'

'I was so frightened with all the fuss, and sleepy too, sir. And I never thought John, of all people, would do such a thing. He had nothing against you, sir, only the Beverleys.'

'That's quite enough,' snapped Charles. 'You, boy, what have you to say for yourself?'

Freddy twisted his apron and looked at him dumbly.

'Speak,' commanded the general.

'It were her,' blurted out the boy, jerking a thumb at the housekeeper. 'Her told me I was to say I'd seen 'im.'

'Were you in this plot with John?' demanded Charles wrathfully.

'Oh, no, no, no,' wailed the housekeeper.

Miss Trumble's level voice sounded in the room. 'I think the poor woman was drunk and could not remember much of what happened.'

'I swear I only had a little gin and hot to soothe my nerves, sir,' screeched the housekeeper. 'It was John who told me all about standing next to me. I swear on my mother's grave. He told me Freddy was there as well, so I told the boy what to say, him being not right in the head.'

She began to cry noisily and Charles looked at her with a sort of angry pity. 'Go away and we will talk later,' he said.

When the housekeeper had made a noisy and lachrymose exit, followed by the boy, the company looked at one another.

'I think we should ask in Hedgefield whether John was seen talking to anyone,' said Charles. 'I cannot believe a servant would go to such lengths on his own behalf.' He turned to Barry. 'Perhaps you could ask around.'

133

Barry touched his forehead and left the room.

'This should put an end to the hauntings now that the wretched creature is dead,' said Minerva, stifling a yawn.

'Only if the malice was all his own,' retorted Miss Trumble.

'I think I will take the children outside again, if I may,' said Rachel.

'Such a good idea.' Minerva rose and smoothed down her skirts.

Charles, sharply anxious for the welfare of his children, who were looking frightened, suddenly could not bear them to be subjected to Minerva's brand of 'motherly' concern, and said, 'Do go along with Mark and Beth, Miss Rachel. Miss Santerton and I have much to discuss.'

Minerva sat down again, a little triumphant smile on her lips.

'I will come with you, Rachel.' Miss Trumble headed for the door.

'Could do with some fresh air myself,' said the general.

Lady Beverley stood up. 'Your arm, General. We will *all* go.'

'Sit down, Father, and Miss Trumble. We shall all discuss this affair,' said Charles and then added innocently, 'but go along with your daughter by all means, Lady Beverley.'

'On second thoughts,' said Lady Beverley,

134

'I feel perhaps my place is here.' She sat down again.

'Well, I'm bored with the whole thing,' drawled George Santerton. 'Such a lot of fuss over a mere footman.'

'And, sure, I am shaken to the core of my poor old body,' complained Mrs. Kennedy. 'I for one am going home.'

'You are a brave lady,' said the general. 'What an experience! I will escort you out to your carriage.'

Miss Trumble, half-amused, half-exasperated, saw the sudden alarm and consternation on Lady Beverley's face as the general tenderly escorted Mrs. Kennedy to the door.

Rachel had already gone. Minerva kept turning that intense blue gaze of hers on Charles. Miss Trumble wondered whether Minerva's ambition to be mistress of Mannerling, for such an ambition was very obvious, would ever be fulfilled. But then, men were so silly when it came to pretty women.

*　　*　　*

Rachel walked with Mark and Beth towards the folly. She wondered what to say to them. They admittedly lived in violent times and there was death all about them on every gibbet they passed. But the sight of a body plummeting from the roof of Mannerling, to die at their feet, was enough to shake an adult, let alone two vulnerable children. Rachel was beginning to feel rather sick and shaken herself. It was not only the death of John but that he had been prompted by such evil malice. Even if someone had been paying him, it had been an evil thing to do to carry out such orders.

'We will take the boat out on the lake,' she said, 'and we will talk a little bit about what has happened.'

The children, who normally would have treated such an offer with noisy joy, followed her silently down the grassy slope to the jetty. They sat side by side, facing her as she slotted the oars into the rowlocks and began to pull steadily away from the jetty.

'You are both very brave children,' began Rachel. 'After we have spent some time on the water, we will return and have something to eat and then I think you should both go to bed. I am very shaken and tired myself.'

Beth began to cry and Mark put an arm round her. Tears welled up in his own eyes. Rachel shipped the oars, took out a handkerchief, and began to cry herself.

At last, she firmly dried her eyes and said with a shaky laugh, 'Now I feel better. But think on it, Mark, I was going to play at pirates, but we don't look very ferocious, any of us.'

With children's lightning changes of mood, both stopped crying. 'Real pirates?' asked Beth cautiously.

'Yes. I tell you what. If you want to be real pirates, you must learn to row. I know the oars are rather big, but you could take an oar each.'

She rowed back to the jetty. She changed places with the children. 'Now, you are the wicked Turkish pirates and I am your hostage.'

'You don't look like a hostage,' pointed out Mark. 'You should be bound and gagged.'

'I saw some string under a bench in the folly,' said Rachel.

She tied up the boat again. Soon she was bound with string and gagged with her scarf. The children gingerly rowed away from the jetty. At first they went round in circles because Mark was pulling more strongly than Beth, but they finally managed some sort of co-ordination.

Rachel was soon beginning to tire of playing the part of hostage, straining at her bonds and making gurgling noises from behind her scarf, but the children were so enraptured with this new skill of rowing that she did not have the heart to call an end to their play—which she very well could, for the scarf over her mouth was quite loosely tied.

And so that was how Charles Blackwood saw them as he paused in the folly and looked down on the lake. His children were uttering quite dreadful oaths and threats to the bound and gagged Rachel.

He strode out of the folly and down to the lake.

He hailed Mark, crying, 'You'd best come ashore. The sky is darkening and I think it is going to rain.'

At first they spun in circles, both children being anxious to show off their prowess to their father, but at last they managed to reach the jetty, just as Charles was joined by Miss Trumble.

'We were playing pirates,' said Mark, his voice squeaky with excitement, 'and Rachel is our hostage.'

Rachel said plaintively from behind her scarf, 'Would someone please untie me?'

Charles knelt down on the jetty and untied the scarf and then her hands, and Rachel untied her ankles.

Miss Trumble helped Mark and Beth out of the boat and said briskly, 'Come along. You will eat and go to bed, and if you are very good, I will read a story to you.'

They went off with her, still chattering excitedly. Charles helped Rachel out.

'You are very good, Miss Rachel,' he said, beginning to walk with her.

'I like your children,' said Rachel. 'We have all had a bad fright.'

A fat drop of rain struck the back of Charles's hand. He looked at the sky and said, 'Let us shelter in the folly for a little. I think it will only prove to be a shower.'

As they reached folly, the heavens opened.

138

They stood together, looking out, surrounded on all sides by a silvery curtain of rain. 'The children will be soaked,' said Rachel.

Charles laughed. 'Did you not notice the estimable Miss Trumble was carrying an umbrella?' Then he studied her thoughtfully.

'I do not want to distress you, Miss Rachel,' said Charles, 'but you know the recent history of Mannerling. The house appears to take hold of people in a strange way. Can you think of anyone who would go to such lengths to scare me away, or do you think that footman was deranged?'

Rachel felt guilty. For who could know better about an obsession to gain Mannerling than the Beverleys?

'It is difficult for me to speculate on the subject,' she said in a low voice. 'You must have heard the gossip about us. Mr. Judd was obsessed with the place, as was Harry Devers. But both are dead and I know of no others.'

He gave her a slanting look from those green eyes. 'And the Beverleys are no longer obsessed?'

'No,' she said in a half-whisper.

'I am sorry to pain you, but it is all too evident that Lady Beverley is setting her cap at my father.'

Rachel felt immeasurably tired. She was intensely aware of his masculinity, of his attraction. But also that she did not stand a chance with such a man because of such a mother and such a reputation.

'Mama has not been quite ... right ... since the loss of Mannerling and is apt to be a trifle silly on the subject,' she said stiffly. 'But Mama would never do anything to hurt your children, nor would I or my sisters.'

He gave a sigh. 'It is all very strange. Mr. Cater seemed much taken with the house. What do you know of him?'

'Only what he has told me, that he is a sugar-plantation owner, here in England on a visit. Yes, he wishes to settle here. But just suppose he craved to get possession of Mannerling. How would he know that John out of all the other servants would prove such an easy tool?'

'Who told him of Mannerling?'

'A Lord Hexhamworth, an old friend of my father.'

'Mr. Cater resides at the Green Man in Hedgeworth, I believe. How long does he plan to remain there?'

'I do not know. I will ask him, if you wish. He is a frequent caller.'

'Oho, and why is that?'

Rachel blushed.

'He is a good catch,' said Charles, looking at her with affectionate amusement.

There had still been a little spark of hope in Rachel's heart until that last comment. Now there was no hope at all.

'It has stopped raining,' she said in a stifled voice.

'So it has, and look, over there, a rainbow.'

They walked back to the house together. He chatted easily of this and that, looking all the while curiously at her sad, averted face.

'I am sorry if I distressed you by seeming to accuse your family of being behind these hauntings. You must forgive me and realize I have been overset at what I see as a threat to my children. Come, now, Miss Rachel, and smile at me. What would I have done without you to bring their plight to my attention?'

He stopped and looked down at her. She gave him a watery smile and then began to cry.

He took out his handkerchief and, tilting up her face, gently dried her tears. 'I am the veriest brute to distress you so. We both need some tea and something to eat.'

He linked his arm in hers and Rachel walked beside him, feeling the strength of that arm, her body a tumult of mixed emotions.

Minerva stood at the window with her brother beside her and watched their approach.

'Pretty picture,' sneered George.

'What am I to do about that wretched girl?' demanded Minerva.

'Why do you always ask me what you are to do? You're always accusing me of being stupid.'

'When you are not stupid in drink and all about in your upper chambers, brother dear,

141

you have some ideas.'

'I did hear in Hedgefield that the Cater fellow was courting Rachel.'

Minerva brightened. 'Perhaps that might be the answer.'

'Not if little Miss Rachel thinks she can get Charles and Mannerling as well.'

'A bribe to Cater might answer.'

George shrugged. 'You can try, but the fellow's supposed to be as rich as Croesus.'

'It has been my experience that no matter how much money people have, they are always ready to accept more.'

'You can try. I have had too much excitement for today. Do you join the others to dine?'

'And see Rachel making sheep's eyes at Charles and the mother flirting grotesquely with the general? Not I. I think I will search out this Mr. Cater. Order the carriage for me.'

'Order it yourself,' complained her brother. 'The house is full of servants. They didn't all fall off the roof.'

*   *   *

Mr. Cater returned to the Green Man after a brisk ride across the local countryside to learn that a lady was waiting for him.

Minerva noticed the way his face fell when he saw her and experienced a spasm of irritation.

142

'I beg your pardon, ma'am,' he said. 'I was somehow expecting to see Miss Rachel Beverley.'

Was every man besotted with that wretched girl? Minerva gave him a thin smile. 'We met briefly, if you remember, Mr. Cater. At Mannerling.'

'Yes, indeed, Miss Santerton. And what is the reason for this very highly flattering call?'

'I thought we should have a comfortable coze about our ambitions.'

'I am a happy man. I do not think I have any ambitions at the moment.'

'Perhaps I am mistaken. Rumour has it you are courting Rachel Beverley.'

'If that be the case,' he said gently, sitting down opposite her in the coffee-room. He signalled to the waiter and then ordered a glass of shrub. When the waiter had departed, he went on. 'If that be the case, then it is not something I would discuss freely. It would be ... er ... my private business.'

A flash of irritation, quickly masked, crossed Minerva's face. This was all going to be much more difficult than she had imagined. 'I see I will have to put all my cards on the table.' She gave a little shrug. 'Why not? I understand you to be interested in gaining the hand of Rachel Beverley and the ownership of Mannerling.'

The waiter put a glass of shrub at Mr. Cater's elbow. Mr. Cater took a meditative sip.

'I can dream,' he said.

'But do you not see, it could be a reality?' Minerva leaned forward. 'And I am the person to help you.'

'Why, Miss Santerton? You barely know me.'

'I am interested in securing Mr. Charles Blackwood for myself—in marriage.'

'And what is that to do with me?'

'Mr. Blackwood is becoming uncommonly interested in Rachel Beverley and he is the owner of Mannerling.'

'In which case, Miss Rachel would regain her old home without my help.'

She gave a little click of impatience. 'You do not strike me as a stupid man, Mr. Cater.' She began to gather up her reticule and pull on her gloves.

'No, stay, you interest me, Miss Santerton. If I remove the affections of Miss Rachel away from Mr. Blackwood, how would that gain me Mannerling?'

'Without such competition, Charles would wed me and I would persuade him to remove from Mannerling. He is already upset about the place. I think the death of that footman might have been the last straw.'

'What footman?' demanded Mr. Cater sharply.

'I cannot remember his name. Mrs. Kennedy of Perival found a livery button on the roof and assumed that whoever had been haunting Mannerling was the owner of the button. This footman came up behind her and tried to seize it and she pushed him off the roof. Amazing! An old woman like that! Why, you are a trifle pale, Mr. Cater. It was only a footman.'

'I do not like to hear of any man's death. There was really no reason for you to go to this trouble. I do not anticipate any difficulty over my courtship of Rachel Beverley. The family is in need of money and I gather she has little dowry to speak of, unless, of course . . .'

His voice tailed off.

'Unless, of course,' Minerva finished for him, 'Charles Blackwood gets there first.'

'Is there any danger of that?'

'I do not think there is any immediate danger. I heard rumours, I sense that Mr. Blackwood's last marriage was not a happy one. That will make him cautious. But Rachel has a clever ally.'

'That being?'

'Miss Trumble, her governess, a sharp and scheming woman. She places Rachel like a chess piece neatly in Charles's way on all occasions. Charles's father is becoming enamoured of this governess.'

'So what do you suggest, O wise Miss Santerton?'

'I would suggest you approach the mother, Lady Beverley, without delay, and gain her permission to pay your addresses to her daughter.'

He regarded her shrewdly. 'What if I told you I was not interested in either Miss Rachel or Mannerling?'

Minerva smiled at him sweetly. 'I would not believe you.'

He smiled back. 'And what do I get if I do as you bid?'

'You get my help and a large sum of money.'

His eyes raked over her and he leaned back in his chair. 'I have no need of money. Perhaps you could reward me in other ways.'

'We will pretend that was never said.' Minerva rose to her feet. 'I made a mistake.'

'No, no, please be seated. I jest, and rather crudely, too. My sincere apologies.'

Minerva sat down slowly. 'Do you know who was behind those hauntings at Mannerling?'

'This footman, surely.'

'A mere footman would not go to such lengths. Someone was paying him.'

'If you say so. I have no interest in what goes on at Mannerling.'

'Only in the house itself?'

'Yes, it fascinates me. I often dreamt of it.'

'Why? When you had never seen it till you came here.'

'Someone told me of it, in Barbados, where I sweated under the sun and dreamt of England. I came expecting the place to be nothing out of the common way and fell under its spell.'

'I have heard of the enchantment of Mannerling,' said Minerva. 'But to me, it is only a house, and one that is too far from the delights of London for my taste. So do we agree to help each other?'

He held out his hand. She took it in her own and he shook it. 'Remember the governess,' she warned. 'She will make trouble for you.'

'Why? I am a good parti.'

'A feeling. Make your proposal and we will see.'

*   *   *

Mr. Cater dressed carefully in his best the following day and rode over to Brookfield House. The weather was warm but wet and he learned from the maid who took his hat and gloves that the young ladies were abovestairs in the schoolroom with the Mannerling children and their governess. He said he had come to see Lady Beverley.

Fortunately for Mr. Cater, it was not one of Lady Beverley's many 'sick' days. She received him in the drawing-room, which smelt of damp and disuse.

'Mr. Cater,' said Lady Beverley after that gentleman had refused an offer of refreshment, 'we are extremely glad to see you on this inclement day. Shall I summon my daughters?'

'Not yet. I am here to ask your permission to pay my addresses to Miss Rachel.'

'I did not expect this, sir!'

'You must have noticed that my attentions to your daughter were particular.'

'My daughters are so beautiful that I am accustomed to gentlemen paying them particular attention. Rachel is a pearl above price.'

By which she means, thought Mr. Cater cynically, that there is no dowry worth mentioning.

'I am a very rich man, my lady,' he said, 'and would be able to furnish your daughter with every comfort. I understand'—here he gave a delicate cough—'I have been warned that there is little dowry but I am not interested in mere money.'

Lady Beverley smiled on him fondly. 'Well, well,' she said indulgently. 'We must not rush matters. We will see what Rachel has to say to the matter, but I cannot think of anything against your suit. Our respective lawyers will deal with tiresome things like marriage settlements. Excuse me for a moment.'

She swept out, leaving the door ajar. Lady Beverley met Miss Trumble on the stairs. 'Such news,' she cried. 'You must fetch Rachel immediately. Mr. Cater has asked my permission to pay his addresses to her.'

Miss Trumble went very still. 'I trust you did not give your permission, or rather, not yet.'

'Are your wits wandering, woman? This is a rich planter. I will fetch Rachel myself.'

To her amazement, Miss Trumble barred her way.

'Step aside! You forget yourself!'

'No, stay, my lady, listen to me. What do we really know of this Mr. Cater? He says he is a rich planter, but we have only his word for it. Rich men usually stay at private homes, having secured letters of introduction. He says that Lord Hexhamworth had told him of Mannerling, and yet he carries no letter from him. I have written to friends to find out what I can and await their reply. Do not turn him down, but tell him to give you time.'

'You silly woman. The man is richly dressed and his horses are the talk of the neighbourhood.'

'Who knows he even paid for them?' demanded the governess. 'What if your daughter wed him and then disappeared, to be never heard of again? The Beverleys have suffered enough scandal. You cannot promise your daughter to a man whose background we know nothing of and who is staying at a common inn. I only beg a little more time, my lady. Only think how you would sink in General Blackwood's esteem if you were party to a misalliance for you daughter!'

'Perhaps I have been too hasty,' said Lady Beverley. 'I will be cautious. Find out what you can.' She turned and went back down the stairs.

Mr. Cater retreated quickly from the

doorway of the drawing-room, where he had been listening intently to the conversation on the stairs. Damn that poxy governess. Something would have to be done.

Lady Beverley returned. Mr. Cater listened as she said that she had been too hasty in accepting his proposition. Give it a little more time and get to know Rachel better, urged Lady Beverley.

Mr. Cater received this with every appearance of good grace, secured a promise that he could take Miss Rachel driving on the morrow if the weather was fine, and took his leave.

After he had gone, Lady Beverley paced up and down. She did not like the way this high-handed governess kept taking matters into her own hands. She would watch the post and when any letters arrived for Miss Trumble, she would read them herself and make up her own mind about any news they contained.

*   *   *

Lady Evans received a call from Miss Trumble on the following day. 'Letitia!' she cried. 'You are welcome.'

Miss Trumble say down and heaved a little sigh. 'Have any letters arrived for me in care of you?'

'Two. I planned to send them over today by the footman. Not that I mind you using this

150

address, Letitia, but why?'

'Lady Beverley often thinks it is part of her position to open letters addressed to her daughters. I do not want her to look at mine. May I see them?'

Lady Evans went to an escritoire in the corner and picked up two letters and handed them to Miss Trumble.

'You will excuse me for a moment.' Miss Trumble opened the letters and scanned them swiftly. 'No, they do not contain news of the mysterious Mr. Cater but of the Santertons. There is not much. Only that business about the late Mr. Santerton having died under mysterious circumstances. Minerva is considered of flighty temperament and given to outbursts of rage. But the general opinion is that she had nothing to do with her husband's death. All hysterical gossip fuelled by the lady's unpopularity in her county. Nothing really that I did not know already. I am awaiting news of Mr. Cater.'

'Why?'

'He wishes to propose to Rachel.'

'Then she is very lucky. He is rich and handsome.'

'And unknown. And residing at the Green Man and not at a private residence. I must find out more. Have you heard the news of the death at Mannerling?'

'The footman? Yes, that Irish aunt of Fitzpatrick's was amazing brave.'

'She is an exceptional lady.'

'So what is behind the trouble at Mannerling, unless this footman was simply deranged?'

'That I do not know. Perhaps that wretched house has put its spell on the Santertons and they are trying to scare Charles Blackwood out of it, and yet Minerva obviously wants to marry him, in which case she would get Mannerling as well.'

'I heard something of Charles Blackwood's marriage,' said Lady Evans.

'Indeed? What was it?'

'Only rumours that his late wife was too free with her favours, and among her own servants, too.'

'That might explain a certain sadness and reserve in him.'

'Are you scheming to get him for one of your girls?'

'I never scheme.'

'And are you not supposed to be instructing the Mannerling children?'

'Not today. Their father has taken them to some fair. Do you think it will rain?'

'I do not think so.'

'Pity.'

'Why? You do not want to get wet on the road home.'

'I just wanted to know that someone's drive might be curtailed.'

'Miss Rachel,' Mr. Cater was saying, 'did your mama mention to you that I wish to pay my addresses to you?'

Rachel looked at him, startled. 'No, sir.'

'But it would not distress you?'

Rachel gazed down at her hands. Here was a chance of a good marriage to a rich and handsome man. It was unusual that her mother had not leaped at the offer. Charles's face seemed to rise up before her.

'What did my mother say?'

'Lady Beverley suggested we give it a little more time.'

'I think that is very wise,' said Rachel, her heart beginning to beat hard and her head full of confused and muddled thoughts.

'I have plans,' he said slowly, 'great plans. I have decided to return to the Indies soon and sell my property and settle in England. I need a good house, good land ... and a wife.'

'I am very honoured—very flattered,' said Rachel. 'I realize you would like an answer before you return. Give me some time to think.'

'As you will. But may I make a suggestion?'

'Certainly.'

'I feel that spinster of a governess has too much influence on your family. I would not discuss this with her.'

'Miss Trumble is kind and wise.'

153

'But what can a shrivelled-up old spinster know of marriage?'

'I am sorry,' said Rachel stiffly. 'I will brook no criticism of Miss Trumble.'

'You must forgive me then. I am anxious to secure you.'

Rachel cast a quick little sideways glance at his face. Perhaps, she thought, if he had claimed to be in love with her, had taken her in his arms, she might have been swayed. But there seemed nothing of the lover about him. They had reached Brookfield House. Rachel reluctantly offered him refreshment. He was about to accept when he saw Miss Trumble come out of the house and stand on the doorstep, awaiting their arrival. Her eyes were shrewd and assessing as she looked at him. He shook his head and declined Rachel's offer.

'I have been waiting for you,' said Miss Trumble, following Rachel into the house. 'Did Mr. Cater propose to you?'

Rachel nodded. 'I asked him to give me a little more time, although he appears anxious to get an answer soon. He returns soon to the Indies and plans to sell up and buy a property in England.'

'Interesting,' said Miss Trumble.

'Do you think I should accept?'

'That is for you to decide, Rachel, but we do not know anything about him, really, or his family, or his background. Perhaps we will find out something soon.'

There was a rumble of carriage wheels outside. Miss Trumble went back to the doorway and looked out. 'Why, it is Mr. Blackwood and the general and the children.'

Rachel went out with her. Her heart lurched as she saw Charles. Was she really becoming enamoured of him, or was it because of Mannerling?

Miss Trumble welcomed them all and ushered them into the parlour and then went to fetch her mistress. The children were bubbling with excitement over their day at the fair. Beth sat on Rachel's lap and Mark at her feet as with shining eyes they described their day.

'Now, now,' she interrupted them at last. 'Let me remove my bonnet and gloves. I am just this minute returned from a drive.'

Lady Beverley, Belinda, Lizzie, and Miss Trumble entered the room just in time to hear Rachel's last sentence.

'Ah, you had a pleasant time with Mr. Cater, I hope?' asked Lady Beverley. She turned to the general. 'Mr. Cater is desirous of wedding our little Rachel, but our stern governess demands caution. But then elderly spinsters were always cautious, were they not?'

'Mama!' protested Lizzie.

Charles looked sharply at Rachel. He had always thought her a pretty girl, but far too young for him, and then that Beverley obsession with Mannerling was always at the back of his mind. But there was something so lovable about her, so vulnerable, as she sat there with Beth on her knees and Mark at her feet.

She looked up then and met his eyes and found herself trapped in his gaze. Her cheeks flushed pink.

'And did you accept the proposal?' asked Charles.

'I do not know what to do,' said Rachel. 'I think it would be better to wait a little to find out more about our Mr. Cater.'

Rachel urged Beth down onto the floor next to Mark, for her legs had begun to tremble under that gaze. She was intensely aware of him and at the same time frightened to look at him again.

'So how do you go on, Miss Trumble?' asked the general. 'You should have been with us this day to keep these unruly brats in order.'

'You should have asked me to accompany you, dear General,' said Lady Beverley just as if she had never damned fairs as vulgar. 'I am excellent with children.'

As she never even looked at Mark or Beth or talked to them, the general wondered if she had even had much conversation with her own daughters.

He was irritated with Lady Beverly and he had not liked that remark about elderly spinsters one bit.

'We should be pleased to see you at Mannerling soon, Miss Trumble,' said the general. 'The gardens are looking very fine.'

'The gardens were always accounted beautiful,' said Lady Beverley before Miss Trumble could reply. 'And yes, we would be delighted to accept your invitation. Would tomorrow be suitable?'

The general rolled his eyes at his son, but Mark cried excitedly, 'Please say you'll come, Rachel. We can have such larks!'

'It is up to your father,' said Rachel quietly.

'Miss Rachel to you, Mark,' said Charles, sounding half-amused, half-exasperated. 'Oh, very well. I shall send the carriage for you all at three.'

'Unfortunately, Miss Trumble will be needed here.' Lady Beverley smoothed the folds of her gown, a hard little smile on her face.

'In that case,' said the general, 'we will leave it until Miss Trumble is free.'

'What is it that you wish Miss Trumble to do?' asked Rachel. 'Perhaps I could stay behind and help.'

'Now I come to think of it,' said her mother, throwing her a baffled look, 'it was but a trifling matter and can wait until another day. Yes, we are pleased to accept your invitation, Mr. Blackwood.'

They rose to take their leave. The girls and Lady Beverley walked out to the carriage with them.

Charles took Rachel's hand in his and bent

157

and kissed it. 'Until tomorrow,' he said. She felt a surge of sheer gladness rush through her body. She smiled at him suddenly, a blinding, bewitching smile. He smiled back until an impatient little cough from Lady Beverley brought him to his senses and he realized he was holding her hand in a tight grip.

After they had gone, Rachel went up to her room and locked the door. She wanted to be alone with her thoughts.

*   *   *

Mr. Cater was in the drawing-room at Mannerling. 'You had the right of it,' he said to Minerva. 'She has not accepted my proposal ... yet ... and I know it is all the fault of that governess. Rachel don't rate her own mother very highly, but she dotes on that shrivelled bag of bones.'

'Such an *old* woman,' cooed Minerva. 'The old are so frail and subject to heart attacks, apoplexies ... and ... er ... *accidents*.'

They both regarded each other for a moment and then Mr. Cater gave a little nod.

Charles entered the room and stopped short at the sight of Mr. Cater.

'My apologies.' Mr. Cater rose to his feet and made his best bow. 'I was passing and called to see you.'

'Do not let me delay your departure,' said Charles stiffly.

'We have had such a comfortable coze,' said Minerva brightly. 'Mr. Cater has proposed to Rachel Beverley.'

'Indeed,' remarked Charles, his face stiff.

'I will walk downstairs with you.' Minerva got up gracefully and looped the lace train of her gown over her arm. Minerva was very fond of trains and Charles wondered if she would ever take her leave or whether Mannerling was to be perpetually haunted by the swish of her gowns on the stairs or along the corridors.

'He looks on me as a rival,' muttered Mr. Cater as they went downstairs. 'I can see it on his face.'

'Then do something about that governess,' hissed Minerva. 'Leave Blackwood to me.'

She turned and went back upstairs. 'Such a charming man, Mr. Cater,' she sighed. 'Rachel Beverley would do very well to marry him. Of course we all know what is holding her back.'

'That being?' demanded Charles moodily.

'I think your intimacy with the Beverleys has raised their hopes of getting back into Mannerling again.'

'I do not think that troubles them any longer.' Charles leaned with one hunched shoulder against a curtain and stared out moodily across the park.

She gave a tinkling little laugh. 'With their ambitious reputation? Do not be so naïve. If the daughter's ambition is not apparent to you, only look at the mother. She would have demanded her daughter marry Mr. Cater were she not so blatantly setting her cap at the general.'

'I have things to attend to.' Charles strode from the room. But the poison she had poured in his ear worked its way into his brain. Had he not suffered enough from having been married to a jade who had only wanted his money?

But he now hated Minerva with a passion for having disillusioned him. The happiness and elation he had felt earlier were all gone. He went in search of his father and found him in the library.

'Father!'

'Hey, m'boy, you look like the devil. What's amiss?'

'I think the Santertons have outstayed their welcome and I am anxious to see them gone.'

'Difficult,' said the general. 'Short of telling 'em bluntly to get out, I don't think you'll move them. Anyway, Minerva Santerton wants you to propose and she'll hang around until all hope is gone.'

'And how is all hope to go?'

'Wouldn't fancy that pretty Rachel, would you?'

'I have no desire to realize the Beverley ambitions of getting Mannerling back.'

'Apart from the mother, I don't think they have any. Tell you what, you could tell Minerva that you are proposing marriage to the Beverley chit. Bet you she leaves prompt.'

'And what if Miss Rachel finds out from Minerva that I am supposed to be about to propose to her?'

'Well, she won't. What's Minerva going to do, hey? Ride over to Brookfield House and make a scene? Hardly. Tell her, my boy, she'll go off, and then you'll be free of the woman and her boring brother.'

Charles paced up and down. 'It might work. I think it might just work. I'll do it!'

* * *

At dinner that evening, Charles said, 'I was taken aback by your remarks about the Beverleys, Miss Santerton.'

'Minerva,' she corrected with a smile.

'You see,' said Charles earnestly, 'I myself have proposed to Rachel and been accepted.'

Minerva's eyes flashed blue fire.

'You said nothing of this!'

'There was really no reason for me to discuss my private affairs,' said Charles.

'But is this official?'

'Not yet,' put in the general. 'Rachel and Charles have got to get to know each other a little better before Lady Beverley calls down the lawyers and marriage settlements on all our heads. It's still all a secret. Pray do not say anything.'

George Santerton had been drinking, as usual, too much before he even sat down to dinner.

'May as well leave tomorrow, sis,' he said sleepily. 'Nothing for you here.'

'I do not know what you are talking about,' snapped Minerva. She had a determined chin and a Roman nose. How odd, thought Charles, that he had not noticed before how prominent her nose was.

'But,' she went on, 'I had intended to announce our immediate departure. May I wish you joy? The Beverleys will be in alt at having their ambitions fulfilled.'

'As to that, if you mean to regain Mannerling, that will not be the case,' said Charles.

'How so?' slurred George.

'I have decided I do not like the place. Is that not so, Father? We plan to sell.'

'That's it, my boy,' said the general, although the sale of Mannerling was news to him.

'And little Miss Rachel knows of this proposed sale?' demanded Minerva, her eyes narrowing.

'Yes,' said Charles, deciding to add one more lie.

'You amaze me.' Minerva picked fretfully at the food on her plate. 'I have the headache. Be so good as to summon my maid. It has been kind of you both to entertain us, but I pine for home and will repair there on the morrow.'

Charles found he was almost feeling sorry

for her as she trailed from the room, another of those long trains of hers swishing across the floor. George Santerton, however, had no intention of leaving the table before he had demolished several more bottles of wine. Charles suppressed a sigh. One more boring evening, but tomorrow he would be shot of the pair of them.

But before Minerva left the dining-room, Mark and Beth, who had been listening outside the door, scampered off up the stairs.

'There you are!' exclaimed Mark when they reached the privacy of his room. 'You said it was wrong to listen at doors, but Papa is to be married, and to our Rachel! And that horrible Minerva woman is leaving.'

'We are not supposed to know,' cautioned Beth.

'Won't say a word. And selling this place! I shall be glad to say goodbye to Mannerling.' Mark lowered his voice. 'This house does not like us.'

'Pooh, that was that footman,' said Beth, but her voice trembled.

'I did not mean to frighten you. I just made that up,' said Mark quickly, proving that he could lie as well as his father.

*   *   *

The last light was leaving the sky as Miss Trumble stood in the garden talking to Barry.

'The sad thing is,' she said, 'that Rachel is very aware of Charles Blackwood and she would be good for his children, but I do not think she has much hope there. He looks on her with affection, it is true, but I fear the scandal about the Beverleys' ambitions will stop his feelings from becoming anything warmer. I told you how I counselled Lady Beverley to wait until I found out more about our Mr. Cater, and yet I am worried that I might be stopping Rachel from seizing hold of a good marriage.'

'And yet there is something about Mr. Cater you do not like?'

'It is not quite that. It is simply that he is not very forthcoming about family or background. But I should hear from my friends quite soon.'

'You have many influential friends, miss.'

'I have worked in many important households. My employers were and still are very kind to me. I must go to bed now. Good night, Barry.'

Barry went to shut the hens up for the night and Miss Trumble made her way slowly across the lawn.

The night was very still and quiet. Then an owl flew out of the branch of a cedar tree above her head. She swung round to watch its flight.

And that was when she saw a black masked figure in the moonlight, racing across the garden towards her, cudgel raised.

For one second she stood still in amazement and then, with an agility surprising in one so

164

old, she picked up her skirts and ran, screaming 'Help!' at the top of her voice.

Barry darted out of the hen-house, saw the distant flutter of Miss Trumble's skirts as she rounded the house, saw the pursuer, and with a great roar began to run, grabbing a spade as a weapon.

Miss Trumble's pursuer heard the thud of feet behind him and swung round, cudgel raised. Barry stood panting, his spade at the ready. Miss Trumble's cries could now be heard from inside the house.

The man lunged at Barry, who jumped nimbly back and then swung his spade, catching the man on the hip. He grunted with pain and turned and began to run, Barry after him. As he reached the brook that ran along the boundary of the garden, Barry swung the spade again and brought it down on the man's head. He stumbled and fell face down in the brook.

Barry stopped, turned him over, and ripped off the mask. In the brief glimmer of light before the moon was obscured by the cloud, he found himself looking down at a face he did not know.

Josiah, the one-legged cook, was making his way across the grass, holding a lantern. Barry turned. 'Bring the light here,' he called.

But just as he turned, the man on the ground leaped to his feet and ran off through the brook and over the fields beyond like a hare. Barry swore under his breath and set off after him again, but the clouds were gathering overhead and the night was black, and soon he realized he had lost him.

When he returned to the house, it was to find everyone awake.

'I lost him,' said Barry to Miss Trumble, who was being comforted by Rachel.

'Did you get a look at him?' asked Miss Trumble.

'I took off his mask. Never saw the fellow before. Must have been some footpad. I'll need to ride to Hedgefield and rouse the constable and the militia.'

'Do not be away all night,' cautioned Lady Beverley. 'You are to act as footman on the visit to Mannerling on the morrow and we will all need our sleep.'

'Really, Mama,' protested Lizzie. 'Miss Trumble could have been killed. The man may come back.'

'I'll go to the farm and get farmer Currie to send two fellows over to keep guard while I am gone,' said Barry. 'And Josiah has the shotgun primed.'

Rachel finally helped Miss Trumble upstairs to bed. 'Who would attack you?' asked Rachel again. 'Did someone think you were the mistress of the house?'

Miss Trumble sat down wearily on the bed.

'I do not know.' For some reason she kept remembering urging Lady Beverley not to accept Mr. Cater's proposal, remembering now that she was sure she had heard footsteps from the drawing-room downstairs, retreating from the door. But to think that a rich gentleman such as Mr. Cater would pay some thug to attack her was surely far-fetched.

'Tell me, Rachel,' she said, 'what do you think of Mr. Cater?'

'He is all that is pleasant and he is extremely suitable, and yet...'

'What is it?'

'Just something. Perhaps the thought of going abroad and leaving you all. He talks of selling up in the Indies and returning here, but perhaps that might not happen. Do you think I should accept him?'

'I cannot give you an answer yet. Give me a little more time. I would like to know more about him. I will do very well now, child. Go to bed. Lady Beverley will want us all to look our best for the visit.'

Rachel went to her own room, wishing she did not feel so dragged down, wishing somehow that she could accept Mr. Cater's proposal, for she was sure she would never receive another.

Certainly not one from Charles Blackwood!

CHAPTER SIX

Whoever loves, if he do not propose
The right true end of love, he's one that
* goes*
To sea for nothing but to make him sick.

JOHN DONNE

With the exception of Lady Beverley, who was in high spirits, it was a subdued party who set out the following afternoon.

Miss Trumble was heavy-eyed and Belinda and Lizzie worried. Rachel was thinking about seeing Charles Blackwood again and willing herself to discover that he was not out of the common way so that she could settle her mind and marry Mr. Cater.

It was a fine day, with large fluffy clouds sailing across a blue sky. To Rachel's delight, she recognized the carriage from Perival outside the porticoed front of Mannerling.

Mark and Beth ran out to meet Rachel as she descended from the carriage, their eyes shining with excitement.

'Well, you two look very happy,' said Rachel, stooping to give Beth a kiss.

'It's our secret,' crowed Mark. 'And the Santertons have left.'

'When?' demanded Lizzie.

'This very morning.'

'I wonder what made them finally go,' mused Belinda.

'Rachel knows,' said Mark with a grin.

Rachel looked at him sharply. 'No, I don't!'

Mark put a finger to his lips. 'Nearly forgot. Big secret.'

They went into the house and up to the drawing-room, where Isabella and Mrs. Kennedy were already seated with Charles and the general.

'And how do you go on?' the general asked Miss Trumble.

Before the governess could speak, Rachel said, 'Poor Miss Trumble. She was nearly killed last night.'

'Hey, what?' demanded the general, looking startled. There was a babble of excited questions. Lady Beverley frowned majestically, not liking Miss Trumble to be the centre of attention.

Miss Trumble told of her adventures in a calm, level voice.

'But who would dare do such a thing?' demanded the general.

'We live in troubled times,' said Miss Trumble. 'The constable and the militia are scouring the area. I believe Mr. and Miss Santerton are left?'

Mark let out a chuckle of laughter and Beth said, 'Shhh!'

'Yes, they had been here for some time,' said

Charles easily. 'I believe Miss Santerton missed the delights of London.' He turned to Mrs. Kennedy. 'And how are you after your adventures?'

'Very well,' said the Irishwoman. 'But, faith, it's not every day I kill a man.'

'I doubt if we shall ever get to the bottom of that mystery,' said Charles with a sigh.

'And how is Mr. Cater?' asked Mrs. Kennedy.

'I do not really know the man,' remarked Charles, his eyes resting for a moment on Rachel's flushed face.

'But Miss Santerton knew him.'

'I believe she knew him slightly. Miss Santerton met him when he came here to see the house, and then she entertained him one day recently when he called when I was out.'

'And they were seen together having a long conversation in the Green Man,' pursued Mrs. Kennedy.

Charles looked at her in surprise and the Irishwoman's shrewd eyes twinkled back at him. 'Ah, well, sure she's gone and didn't get the proposal she expected, but she must have lost hope, and I thought that one would never lose hope.'

'Oh, but she learned Papa is to marry someone else,' burst out Mark and then turned red in the face as his father glared at him.

Had it been left at that, the subject would have been changed, for Lady Beverley so much

170

wanted to draw the general's attention to herself, but the general said crossly, 'You must not tell lies, Mark.'

Mark looked at him miserably. 'I don't tell lies! I don't! I was passing the dining-room door with Beth last night and I heard you tell Miss Santerton that you were to wed our Rachel.'

'I am afraid you must have misheard us,' said his father coldly.

Beth sprang to her brother's defence. 'But I heard you too, Papa, and we are in alt to have Rachel as a mama. You did say so.'

Lady Beverley sat opening and shutting her mouth.

Charles groaned inwardly.

'Perhaps I had better explain how such a misunderstanding came to arise. Your arm, Miss Rachel.'

Rachel's heart seemed to have gone straight from heaven to hell in one sickening lurch.

For one dizzying moment, she had thought it might be true, that Charles meant to propose to her, and then she had seen the look on his face and his voice saying he must explain how the misunderstanding had arisen.

'One moment.' Lady Beverley arose. 'You cannot take my daughter for a private discussion without her being strictly chaperoned.'

'I am sure Mr. Blackwood means to take Rachel for a walk in the garden,' said Miss

Trumble quickly.

'Yes, indeed, Mama, I shall do very well. Come along, Mr. Blackwood.' Rachel felt she was in for enough misery without her mother adding to it.

They walked together down the staircase. A footman was up on a tall ladder polishing the crystals of the chandelier in the Great Hall. The sun shining down from the cupola cast the footman's elongated shadow across the hall. The crystals tinkled as he worked among them, they sounded in Rachel's ears like a sort of unkind, mocking laughter. It was in that moment that all her old love of her former home left her. Mannerling stood for Beverley misery and Beverley humiliation.

They walked slowly across the lawns in the direction of the folly. 'How do I begin?' said Charles at last. 'You must understand my distress and increasing dislike of having the Santertons resident under my roof. It was not only obvious to me but to everyone else that Miss Santerton thought she had only to wait at Mannerling for as long as she could and a proposal of marriage would be inevitable. Last night my father suggested a ruse to get rid of them. He suggested I tell them that I was betrothed to you in secret. The plot worked, but my wretched children were listening at the door. Please accept my humble apologies.'

They had reached the folly and stood

together looking down at the waters of the lake.

'You have been a good friend to my children,' Charles went on when she remained silent. 'And when we leave Mannerling for a new direction, I will write to you, if I may, and tell you how they go on.'

'By all means,' said Rachel in a voice husky with unshed tears. Then she looked at him, startled, as the full import of his words sank in. 'You plan to sell Mannerling?'

'As soon as possible.'

Rachel gave a little shiver, although the day was warm.

Then she said bravely, 'I accept your apology, Mr. Blackwood. I am glad this misunderstanding has been cleared up. I do not plan to tell my fiancé of it.'

It was his turn to look startled. 'Your fiancé?'

'Yes, Mr. Cater,' said Rachel. 'I have decided to accept him.'

'I hope you will be very happy. Shall we return to the house?'

The grass was starred with daisies and Rachel felt she had counted every one in her path, for she kept her eyes firmly on the grass, frightened that if she looked at him, he would see the hurt and loss in her eyes.

Her fair hair was almost silver in the sunlight and a tendril of escaping hair curled on her neck. She looked young and vulnerable.

173

'Will you be happy going to the Indies?' he asked.

'It will be an adventure, sir.'

'And when is the wedding to take place?'

'As to that, there are lawyers to consult. Marriage settlements, all that sort of thing,' said Rachel miserably.

The children flew across the lawns to meet them. 'Is Rachel to be our new mama?' cried Mark.

'No,' said Charles. 'As I explained, it was all a misunderstanding. Miss Rachel is to marry Mr. Cater.'

'She cannot!' said Mark passionately.

'Behave yourself. Both of you go to your rooms and stay there until I decide what to do with you,' roared Charles.

Hand in hand, they trailed off.

'They are only children,' protested Rachel. 'Please do not be harsh with them.'

'I am still embarrassed over my silly lie. I will not be angry with them any more.'

'Such a *silly* lie,' echoed Rachel dismally. She pinned a bright smile of her face and said with as much cheerfulness as she could summon up, 'Do not tell anyone about my engagement to Mr. Cater. I would rather keep it secret until it is official.'

'You may depend on me.'

They walked slowly up the staircase. So Rachel Beverley would wed the suspicious Mr. Cater. Charles scowled suddenly. He did not trust that man. But surely, when all the lawyers got together, the facts about Mr. Cater would emerge. But why should he think that? England abounded in crooked lawyers. Rachel with the delicate features, the blue eyes and fair hair would be transported to the other side of the world, and he would probably never see her again. He had shied clear of her because of the tales of the Beverleys' ambitions to reclaim Mannerling. And yet, she had received the news that he was about to sell the place with no protest, no reaction. Perhaps, he thought cynically, she was hoping a new owner might prove easier prey. And then he thought that unworthy. What was up with him? He wanted to shake her. And, at the same time, he wanted her to shout at him and berate him for having lied about their engagement. He could not guess from Rachel's apparently calm exterior that all she wanted to do was to run away somewhere and cry her eyes out.

When they entered the drawing-room, everyone promptly stopped talking and gazed at them inquiringly. 'I have apologized for any silly misunderstanding,' said Charles with a lightness he did not feel. 'My children should not listen at doors.'

'Where are they?' asked Miss Trumble.

'They have been sent to their rooms.'

'I will go to them.' Miss Trumble rose.

'Might come along as well,' said the general, heaving himself out of his armchair.

Lady Beverley gave an audible click of

annoyance. 'Please do not trouble, General,' said Miss Trumble quickly. 'I think they will need a talk from their governess.'

Isabella covertly studied Rachel's face. Rachel was now laughing at something Mrs. Kennedy was saying. Isabella, who knew her husband's aunt very well, realized that Mrs. Kennedy was telling one of her tall Irish stories to amuse Rachel and let her keep her countenance. But had Rachel been wounded, thought Isabella, through the loss of Mr. Blackwood, or because of the loss of hopes of Mannerling?

*   *   *

Miss Trumble found the children together in Mark's room. 'Now you are in the suds,' she said cheerfully. 'Listening at doors, indeed.'

'But we were so excited when we thought Papa would marry Rachel,' said Beth dismally. 'Now he won't, and he will perhaps find a lady like Miss Santerton instead.'

'Now, you both must have guessed that he did not like Miss Santerton one bit.'

Mark nodded dismally and then said, 'But why does he not like our Rachel?'

'You cannot force your father to wed someone just because you like that person. Were you listening at the dining-room door?'

Beth and Mark exchanged glances and then Mark said defiantly, 'We are sorry. It was all

176

my fault. But it is a bad habit I was wont to indulge in when Miss Terry was our governess. She was always complaining about us and I wanted to know what she was saying.'

'Do not do such a thing again,' said Miss Trumble.

'No, I won't,' promised Mark, 'or Beth either. But it is a such a pity Rachel is to marry Mr. Cater.'

Miss Trumble went very still. 'Where did you come by that idea?'

'Why, Rachel must have told Papa, for he told us so in front of her and she did not correct him.'

Miss Trumble smiled bleakly, her mind racing. She felt she could see it all: Rachel, learning that she had simply been used as a ruse to get rid of the Santertons—for the general had explained the game when Rachel was out walking with Charles—had said she was engaged to Cater to counter her humiliation, had probably even decided to accept Mr. Cater.

Miss Trumble became anxious to escape to Lady Evans and find out if those letters for her had arrived.

She promised to read more about pirates to the children after their lessons on the following day and returned to the drawing-room.

Lady Beverley, hearing of her governess's desire to leave because of a headache, would normally have protested, the ailments of servants being no concern of hers, but she was anxious to remove Miss Trumble from the general's orbit and so agreed, and a carriage was ordered for Miss Trumble.

Once clear of Mannerling, Miss Trumble told the coach man to drive to Hursley Park instead, the home of Lady Evans.

But no letters for her had arrived. Miss Trumble left feeling dejected. She must talk to Rachel as soon as the girl arrived home and beg her to wait a little longer before making her decision.

*　　*　　*

After their guests had left, the general and his son sat in silence. The lamps had not yet been lit and long shadows fell across the drawing-room.

'Well, that's that,' said the general at last. 'I'm sorry, you know, that you did not settle on little Miss Rachel.'

'Just as well,' said Charles gloomily. 'She is to marry Cater.'

'Have a knack of securing rich husbands, those Beverleys. If we're selling this place, maybe Cater will buy it. Seems monstrous keen on Mannerling.'

'And I will always be haunted by the fear that this man none of us knows much about paid my footman to haunt us.'

'Any way of finding out?'

178

'Watch and wait. In fact, I have a mind not to sell Mannerling until the fellow takes himself off, just to make sure.'

'Hey, my boy, what if your suspicions are correct? Rachel Beverley deserves better.'

'I cannot interfere and stop the marriage. I have no right to interfere in her life.'

A footman came in and began to light the oil-lamps. The general waited until he had left. Then he cleared his throat and said, 'I've been thinking of getting married myself.'

'Miss Trumble?'

His father nodded.

'Normally I would protest strongly at the idea of you marrying a governess, but Miss Trumble is exceptional. She would be very good for Mark and Beth.'

'Just what I thought,' said the general. 'So I have your blessing?'

'Yes, but a word of caution. There is something very grande dame about Miss Trumble. Do not be surprised if she refuses you.'

'Why should she? She's old like me and cannot go on working forever, and that Lady Beverley don't strike me as the sort to take care of an old servant.'

'If she does refuse you,' said Charles, 'see if you can beg her to leave those Beverleys and come to us. The girls are all too old for a governess.'

'I'll do my best, but she'll accept me. No

doubt about that!'

*   *   *

The Beverleys had almost reached home when the Mannerling coach lurched to a halt. Lady Beverley let down the glass. 'Why, it is our Mr. Cater,' she cried, recognizing the planter, who was driving his curricle. 'Do you care to come to Brookfield House and take some refreshment, sir?'

'Thank you, my lady,' said Mr. Cater. 'Perhaps I might have the honour of escorting Miss Rachel home?'

'But it is near dark and the carriage-lamps have been lit!'

Rachel gathered up her reticule. 'I will go with Mr. Cater,' she said. 'It is only a short way.'

Lizzie watched wide-eyed as Rachel left the Mannerling carriage and was helped into Mr. Cater's curricle. 'Never say she is going to accept him, Mama!'

'And why not?' asked Lady Beverley. 'He is a good parti.'

'But she would be so far away and we would not know how she fared,' wailed Lizzie.

'Tish, letters arrive from all over the world.'

'So you have given up hopes of Mannerling?' asked Belinda.

'Not I,' said Lady Beverley with a little smile.

'But you heard Mr. Charles,' protested

180

Lizzie. 'If he had any interest in Rachel at all, he would not have used her in that heartless way to get rid of Minerva and then tell her it was all a hum.'

'That was certainly bad of him,' said her mother. 'But I cannot be at odds with my future stepson.'

'Mama.' Lizzie looked at her uneasily. 'You surely do not believe the general is going to propose to you.'

'I am very sure. I have noticed the way he looks at me.'

Belinda said cautiously, 'But have you not noticed how he favours Miss Trumble?'

'Pah, a man of the general's standing would never propose to a mere governess. No, my chucks, we will soon be back at Mannerling.'

Lizzie noticed that they were now passing Mr. Cater's curricle. Rachel and Mr. Cater could be seen in the light of the carriage-lamps sitting side by side, talking earnestly. She gave a little shiver of dread. Mannerling had made things go wrong again. Mannerling had turned against them. Lizzie always felt Mannerling was a living presence.

*   *   *

'I am delighted you have decided to accept my proposal of marriage,' said Mr. Cater. 'And delighted at your news that Blackwood is to sell Mannerling. I shall make him an offer and beg him to wait until I sell my property in Barbados.'

Rachel felt she should ask him about himself, about his family, but a great weight of depression had settled on her shoulders. 'Shall we discuss this with Lady Beverley tonight?' she realized he was asking her.

'Oh, n-no,' stammered Rachel. 'Not tonight. I am tired. Perhaps tomorrow afternoon?'

'I shall call on you at three o'clock,' he said, 'and then we shall both drive over to Mannerling and get a promise on the property.'

And Charles would think that was the only reason she was marrying Mr. Cater, thought Rachel dismally. And that was when she realized that she did not want to marry Hercules Cater.

Mr. Cater decided to drive back to Hedgefield, rather than be entertained by Lady Beverley, and Rachel was glad to see him go and to escape him after having to endure only a kiss on her hand.

'Rachel!' cried Miss Trumble, who was waiting in the small dark hall for her.

'No,' said Rachel vehemently. 'Not now! I do not want to talk now.'

*   *   *

Charles Blackwood sat in a chair by the window of his bedroom and looked out over

182

the moonlit lawns. Rachel's face kept rising before his mind's eye. The fact that she was to marry Mr. Cater appeared to have focused his thoughts wonderfully. He could think of nothing else. What kind of man was Cater? Charles suspected there was a brutal streak in him. He clutched his hair. How could he have been so blind? Pictures of Rachel playing with his children flitted through his mind, to be then replaced with dark pictures of Rachel being initiated into the mysteries of the marriage bed by Cater.

He could not propose to her himself. Not now. He had told her quite plainly how he had used her name to get rid of the Santertons. What must she think of him?

And yet, her engagement was not official. Had she any feelings for him at all?

He was convinced she was accepting Cater because the man was apparently rich. If only he could talk to her. If only his late wife's memory had not soured him so much.

He had never thought of himself as passionate or impulsive, but now all he wanted to do was to ride over to Brookfield House, get down on his knees, and beg her to accept him before it was too late.

He shifted restlessly in his chair. Perhaps he would get dressed and walk across to the folly and let the fresh night air cool his thoughts.

He dressed hurriedly, without ringing for his servant, putting on only a thin frilled cambric shirt, breeches, and top-boots over his small-clothes, for the night was close and warm.

He walked along the corridor and so down the great staircase of Mannerling. He had come to detest this house, filled as it was with sad memories.

He walked across the daisy-starred lawns under the moonlight to where the slim pillars of the folly shone white against the still waters of the lake.

He leaned against one of the pillars, his heart heavy and sad. There was nothing he could do. He was bound by the fetters of convention. He would need to let events take their course. But how he ached for her and how he realized now what he had lost.

And then an outside sound crept into the noisy tumult of his thoughts. He heard the steady movement of oars on the lake.

He stiffened. Some poacher, no doubt, using his boat to poach fish in his lake!

He strode out of the folly on down to the water's edge.

And then he saw the glimmer of a white gown and the silver shine of fair hair in the moonlight and his heart lurched.

'Rachel!' he called softly. And then louder, 'Rachel!'

A weary little voice reached his ears from across the water.

'Alas, I am caught trespassing again.'

'Come here! Come here to me!'

184

The little boat headed for the jetty.

He went down to meet her.

He had meant to be polite and calm, now that he was sure he had accepted the inevitability of her marriage, but as she reached the jetty, he saw the shine of tears on her face. He bent down and took the painter and secured the boat with shaking hands.

Then he stopped and lifted her bodily from the boat, cradling her in his arms, saying, 'Rachel, oh, Rachel, do not cry, my little love.'

She gave a muffled little sob and wound her arms about his neck and he bent and kissed her mouth, tasting the salt of her tears, kissed her mouth over and over again in the moonlit stillness of the night.

At last he said huskily, 'How could I have been so stupid?' He set her on her feet and stood looking down at her, his hands on her shoulders. 'How did you get here?'

'I walked,' said Rachel. 'I could not sleep. Mr. Cater is to call tomorrow to propose officially. I had not accepted him before, but I was . . . hurt . . . in the way that you had used me to get rid of the Santertons.'

'You must not marry him. We belong together, you and I. Oh, kiss me again, Rachel, and say that you forgive me, that you will marry me.'

'What am I to do?' she said wretchedly. 'Mr. Cater calls tomorrow.'

'Then you must refuse him. It is not official

185

and you are allowed to change your mind. When does he call?'

'At three in the afternoon.'

'I will wait until a little after that and then ask your mother for your hand in marriage.'

'Mama does not know you plan to sell Mannerling,' said Rachel. 'Do not tell her until later.'

'Will it matter very much to you if we do not live here?'

Rachel took a little breath and said firmly, 'I would like to live as far away from Mannerling as possible.'

He kissed her again and caressed her breasts through the thin stuff of her gown until she groaned against his mouth.

At last he said raggedly, 'Let me take you home before I forget myself.' Holding her hand, he led her back across the lawns to the stables. 'Quietly,' he warned. 'I'll saddle up a horse. I do not want the servants to see you.'

Soon, holding her tightly in front of him, he rode out of the Mannerling estate.

When they reached Brookfield House, he dismounted and then lifted her tenderly down from the saddle, kissing her again.

'One more day, my heart, and all will be resolved,' he murmured.

'Oh, Charles, there is one more difficulty.'

'Yes?'

'I fear Mama expects the general to propose to her.'

'Then Lady Beverley is in for a shock. My father is going to propose marriage to your Miss Trumble.'

'Oh, how wonderful. Her future will be secured.'

'If she accepts him. Go in now, Rachel, and dream of me.'

He stood with a smile on his lips as she ran lightly up the short drive and quietly opened the door and let herself in. He waited until he saw the glimmer of a candle in one of the upstairs rooms.

How would Cater take the rejection? he wondered as he rode home.

*   *   *

Barry walked into Hedgefield in the late morning. Miss Trumble had said she needed the carriage to drive to Hursley Park. He had no real business in Hedgefield, but it was market-day and he liked to talk to some of the locals and enjoy a pint of ale at the Green Man.

He walked among the stalls, chatting to various people he knew. He bought a pasty and a mug of salop and stood enjoying the colour and bustle of market-day.

At last he wiped his mouth and decided to go to the Green Man for that pint of ale and then make his way home.

He stood on the threshold of the tap, blinking in the sudden gloom. He sat down at one of the tables and looked around for the waiter.

A man rose from a table in the corner and made his way rapidly to the door, averting his face as he passed Barry.

And all at once Barry was sure the burly man was Miss Trumble's assailant. He got to his feet and hurried to the door. 'Hey, you, fellow!' he cried.

The man glanced over his shoulder and Barry recognized him. He had last seen that face in the brook at home.

The man began to run, with Barry in pursuit. Through the market they raced, Barry shouting, 'Stop! Murderer!' at the top of his voice. Others joined in the chase. Out of Hedgefield ran the man and then veered off the road into the woods. Barry and the other pursuers fanned out, Barry hard behind the fleeing figure. The man was thickset but fleet of foot and might have escaped had he not caught his foot in a rabbit hole and fallen headlong.

In a trice, Barry was on top of him, pummelling him and shouting to the others.

'Now,' he said, as the man was dragged to his feet and held firmly, 'who are you?'

The man looked at him defiantly and then spat on the ground.

Barry punched him full on the nose, and as the man yelped with pain, said grimly, 'That is for a start. Let's begin again. Who are you?'

'Jem Pully.'

'So why did you attack Miss Trumble?'

'Who her?'

Barry drew back his fist again.

'No,' shouted the man, and then mumbled, 'He told me there would be five golden boys in it fer me an' I whacked 'er.'

'Who told you?' demanded Barry with a sudden feeling of dread, a feeling that he already knew the answer.

'Come on,' he urged. 'You can save yourself from the gibbet.'

'Cater,' said the man. 'He said there was this old creature out at Brookfield House, to go and watch and wait and see if I could get 'er on 'er own, like. I went to look out the lie of the land and I sees 'er in the garden.'

'Let's take this one along to the roundhouse,' said Barry, 'and then we'll get hold of Cater.'

But when Jem Pully had been secured in the roundhouse and Barry went to the Green Man, he was told by the landlord that Mr. Cater had ridden out to Brookfield House to propose to Miss Rachel Beverley and had bought drinks for everyone in the tap before he left.

Barry set out for Brookfield House at the head of a crowd of townspeople, hoping he would be in time before something disastrous happened.

*   *   *

Miss Trumble was staring in dismay at two

letters which Lady Evans had handed to her.

'What is the matter, Letitia?' asked Lady Evans. 'You have gone the colour of whey.'

'These letters tell of Mr. Cater,' said Miss Trumble in a thin voice.

'And?'

'And he is half-brother to Ajax Judd, the late owner of Mannerling who hanged himself. And listen to this. He won the plantation in Barbados in a card game with Lord Hexhamworth. Someone who knew him said that Judd had written to him often about Mannerling and he was determined to see the place sometime; in fact, he was about to go there when he learned of his half-brother's death, of the subsequent sale of Mannerling, and at the same time won those plantations.'

'The family surely did not have that much money, apart from what they gained through gambling?'

'No, and the sale of a plantation and slaves might raise enough to buy Mannerling, but what did he plan to live on afterwards?'

'The estates are rich,' said Lady Evans. 'He could raise the rents and milk quite a sum of money from them. But why would he want Rachel Beverley? Such a man would surely want an heiress.'

'Perhaps he has money from other sources.' Miss Trumble stood up. 'I have not seen Rachel since yesterday evening. I must return.'

'But why do you look so frightened and

worried? The man's a gamester, that is all. Not uncommon these days.'

'Because I think he was behind the hauntings. I think he set out to frighten the Blackwoods away from Mannerling. I think he paid that footman to cause trouble, and, worse than that, I think he paid some thug to injure me or kill me, for he feared I would stop Rachel from marrying him.'

'He must be in love with the girl.'

'That is what puzzles me,' said Miss Trumble, heading for the door. 'I don't think he loves her one bit.'

Driving herself, she made her way quickly through Hedgefield, stopping only on the far side when she heard herself being hailed. She recognized Jenny Durton, a laundress, and called on the horse to stop.

'Oh, mum,' cried Jenny breathlessly, 'such goings-on!'

'I am in a hurry to get home, Jenny,' said Miss Trumble.

'They done got that man who tried for to kill you,' gasped Jenny. 'Got him and took him to the roundhouse, Barry and the men. They've all gone to Brookfield.'

'Why?' Miss Trumble clutched the reins tightly.

'Because the man, Jem Pully, he done say that Mr. Cater paid him to hit you, and Mr. Cater's gone to Brookfield to propose to Miss Rachel!'

'Oh, my God!' exclaimed Miss Trumble, and cried to the horse to move on.

*　　　*　　　*

Rachel was feeling ill. She had told her mother that Mr. Cater was coming to propose to her, had told her the night before; and in the morning she had awoken her mother with the news that she was not going to marry Mr. Cater. But she could not impart the glad news that Charles Blackwood was to propose to her, for Lady Beverley went into strong hysterics and all Rachel could do was retreat. Miss Trumble was out. She would need to deal with Mr. Cater herself.

Mr. Cater arrived at Brookfield House in high spirits. His gambler's soul told him that nothing could go wrong now. He remembered his half-brother's last letter to him, in which Ajax Judd had blamed his fall on the humiliation of the Beverleys. 'If only I had married one of those girls,' Mr. Judd had written, 'then Mannerling would have stayed mine.'

Like all gamblers, Mr. Cater was highly superstitious. He was determined to have Mannerling and determined to have Rachel to make sure of keeping the place. Rachel would return with him to the Indies for only so long as it took to sell the place.

And yet, as he drove up the drive and looked

192

at the house, he had a sudden feeling that something *had* gone wrong. There was an air of mourning about the house, no bustle, no chatter of voices, and the little maid who answered the door to him looked cast down.

'I will fetch Miss Rachel,' she said, dropping a curtsy. 'My lady is indisposed.'

She showed Mr. Cater into the drawing-room. He paced up and down. Surely he was worrying about nothing. Lady Beverley was always ill with something or other.

He swung round as the door opened and Rachel came in.

Although she looked very serious, there was a glow about her, a warmth and colour he had not noticed before.

She was wearing a simple high-waisted muslin gown embroidered with blue cornflowers which matched the blue of her eyes. A nosegay of cornflowers was tucked into the blue silk sash of her gown.

'I had expected to see your mother first,' said Mr. Cater heartily. 'Do it right and proper.'

'Please sit down, Mr. Cater,' said Rachel quietly.

He flicked up the tails of his best blue morning coat with the brass buttons.

Rachel sat on a high-backed chair opposite him and clasped her hands together tightly. 'I do not want you to think me flighty, Mr. Cater,' she said, 'but I cannot marry you.'

'What is this? You promised, you gave me

your promise.'

'I am sorry, Mr. Cater, but I cannot marry you.'

'But we belong together. You, me, and Mannerling.'

'As to that,' said Rachel, deciding to lie, 'I do not believe the Blackwoods intend to sell Mannerling.'

His eyes blazed with fury and the veins stood out on his forehead. 'That is your fault!' he cried. 'If you marry me, then Mannerling will be ours.'

'I must repeat, I cannot marry you. I am to marry Mr. Charles Blackwood.'

'You trull. You will get Mannerling and leave me to rot on the other side of the world.'

Rachel stood up and said coldly, 'It is time for you to go, sir.' She walked to the door and held it open.

But although he went to the door, he kicked it shut and locked it.

'Now, Miss Rachel Beverley,' he said, 'you are going to marry me, and when I have finished with you, you will be glad to.'

Rachel darted across the room and put a chair between them, her eyes wide with fright and with dawning knowledge.

'You're mad,' she whispered. 'It was you all along. You paid that footman to drive the Blackwoods out.'

'And a sad mess he made of it,' growled Mr. Cater. He took a step forward. 'Come here.'

Rachel threw back her head and screamed.

Lizzie's voice came from the other side of the door and then the knob rattled. 'Rachel! Rachel!'

'Get Barry!' shouted Rachel. 'Mr. Cater is going to kill me!'

Mr. Cater grabbed the protecting chair from her and threw it across the room. He seized Rachel and dragged her against him.

And then he heard the roar outside and stared over Rachel's shoulder and through the window. Barry Wort was at the head of a mob marching up the drive.

Mr. Cater rushed for the door, unlocked it, savagely punched Josiah, the one-legged cook who had been trying to hammer the door down, ran through the back of the house and out of the kitchen door. Had he run off across the fields, they would have got him, but, made cunning by desperation, he dived into the hen-house and crouched down in the gloom, hearing the pursuit come through the house and out into the back garden, hearing it die away across the fields.

Miss Trumble was comforting Rachel, Lady Beverley was demanding right, left, and centre what had happened, when they heard the sound of horses' hooves and ran to the window in time to see Mr. Cater on horseback fleeing away from Brookfield House.

Charles Blackwood arrived to listen in horror to the story of the assault on Rachel. He immediately rode off in pursuit of Mr. Cater.

When Lady Beverley had calmed down, Miss Trumble carefully explained who Mr. Cater was and of Rachel's escape from his clutches.

'I am sure there must be some mistake,' wailed Lady Beverley. 'Are you sure?'

'There is no mistake, my lady. Mr. Blackwood has gone in pursuit of him.'

'The general is such a brave man.'

'Not the general. Mr. Charles Blackwood.'

'Oh, it is all such a coil,' sighed Lady Beverley. 'More scandal for my poor girls. You should have warned me of this earlier.'

'I did beg you to wait.'

'It is your job to protect my girls, Miss Trumble, and you do not seem to be making a very good job of it.'

Miss Trumble primmed her lips and did not deign to reply.

For the rest of the day and the following night, Charles Blackwood, Barry and the townspeople, the militia and the constable searched for Mr. Cater without success. It was as if he had disappeared into thin air.

*   *   *

Rachel waited anxiously all the following day for Charles to call, but there was no sign of him. Miss Trumble comforted her, saying that he was probably still searching for Mr. Cater.

Mark and Beth had been brought over by the general for their lessons. The general seemed reluctant to leave until Lady Beverley appeared in the schoolroom, where he was seated with Miss Trumble and the children, and said she thought it would be 'fun' for them if she took part in their lessons.

Miss Trumble surveyed her employer with a mixture of exasperation and worry. Sometimes, on one of her 'good' days, it was evident that Lady Beverley had once been as beautiful as her daughters.

But as the general hurriedly said he had to take his leave, the lines of discontent once more marred Lady Beverley's face and she flashed a venomous look at the governess, as if she were the reason for the general's abrupt departure.

The carriage and a footman were sent at four in the afternoon to collect the children, but no Charles and no general.

Rachel, disconsolate, trailed about the garden, where she was joined by Belinda and Lizzie.

'You still look very upset after Mr. Cater's shocking behaviour,' said Lizzie. 'That is why you are so upset, is it not?'

'Yes,' said Rachel, a bleak little monosyllable. She could not bring herself to tell her sisters of her night-time expedition to Mannerling or how Charles had proposed, although she had told Miss Trumble. She thought of her own abandoned and passionate behaviour with a blush. Perhaps he had decided she had loose morals and was not suitable to be his bride. Miss Trumble had told her that his late wife had been considered flighty. Perhaps he thought her the same!

Then she heard the sound of carriage wheels. The colour rose in her face and she ran down the drive to the gate, her eyes shining.

But it was only the general. Lizzie and Belinda joined Rachel as the old man descended stiffly from the carriage. 'No sign of that villain Cater,' he said. 'Charles has just returned and is going to bed. He is exhausted.'

Rachel wanted to weep. He had obviously not thought to call at Brookfield House first to see her, to give her any news ... to propose.

Then she realized the general was saying, 'I am come to see your Miss Trumble. Is she available?'

'I will see,' said Rachel, and went slowly into the house.

She found Miss Trumble in her room and told her that General Blackwood wished to see her.

'Oh dear,' murmured the governess, getting to her feet. 'I may as well get it over with.'

'I hope nothing ails the children,' said Rachel, her voice sharp with alarm.

'No, it is something else.'

'Charles is returned to Mannerling. I thought ... I thought he would call here first.'

'And propose all muddy and exhausted? No,

my child, do not fret. He will be here in the morning.'

Miss Trumble went slowly down the stairs to where the little maid, Betty, was waiting at the bottom.

'I've put the general in the drawing-room, miss,' whispered Betty.

'Very good. Give me ten minutes and then bring in the tea-tray and some of Josiah's seed-cake.'

Miss Trumble went into the drawing-room. Betty went off to the kitchen to tell Josiah to prepare the tea-tray. As she came back into the hall, she found her mistress just descending the stairs.

'Was that a carriage I heard arriving?' demanded Lady Beverley.

'Yes, my lady. General Blackwood is called.'

'Where is he?'

'In the drawing-room, my lady, but—'

Lady Beverley swept past the maid and opened the door of the drawing-room.

And stood stock-still.

General Blackwood was down on one knee before the governess, his hand on his heart.

Lady Beverley backed away quickly and nearly collided with Rachel.

'I have nourished a viper in the bosom of my family,' she cried.

Rachel saw her mother's pale eyes were beginning to bulge, the way they always did before a bout of hysterics.

'Hush, Mama. Come into the parlour and tell us what ails you.'

Lady Beverley wrestled with the desire to spoil the romantic scene in the drawing-room or allow herself the relief of unburdening her shock to her daughters. The unburdening won and she followed Rachel into the parlour.

'The general is proposing to Miss Trumble.'

'It is not so strange,' commented Rachel. 'He has shown himself to be a great admirer of hers.'

'*I* never noticed!'

No, you would not, thought Rachel. She wondered whether to tell her mother about Charles's proposal. But what if he had changed his mind?

'I shall send that serpent packing as soon as the general leaves,' Lady Beverley was saying.

'Oh, I would not do that.' Rachel realized her mother did not know anything about the proposed sale of Mannerling.

'And why not, pray?'

'I would have thought you would be more inclined to be very courteous to Miss Trumble.'

'And why on earth should I be?'

'Because Miss Trumble will be mistress of Mannerling, and if you make an enemy of her, none of us will ever see Mannerling again.'

Lady Beverley opened and shut her mouth like a landed carp while she digested this idea.

'In any case,' went on Rachel smoothly, 'we must not jump to conclusions. Perhaps your eyes tricked you.'

'We will see,' said Lady Beverley grimly.

* * *

'If you think about it, General,' Miss Trumble was saying gently, 'you will find you really don't want to marry me at all. A mere governess, indeed! You must remember what is due to your position.'

The general, now seated in an armchair, said sadly, 'I thought we should suit very well, two old people like us.'

'But you are not in love with me.'

The general turned red. 'Really, Miss Trumble, we are both too old for such emotions.'

Miss Trumble gave a little sigh. 'Perhaps you are right, sir. Why I said that was to underline the fact that your heart is not broken. No one shall know of your proposal.'

The general brightened. He had begun to feel ashamed of having proposed to a servant only to be rejected. Then his face fell. 'But Lady Beverley saw me.'

'And so she did. And so we will tell her that you have decided to amuse the children by having amateur theatricals at Mannerling. You are monstrous fond of theatricals and you were showing me just how well you could play the part of the gallant.'

The general looked at her with all the old

appreciation. 'Demme, ma'am, but you are a pearl above price.'

She gave an amused little nod as Betty entered the room bearing the tea-tray, followed by Lady Beverley.

'I am not interrupting anything, I hope?' demanded Lady Beverley with a thin smile.

'Not at all, my lady,' said Miss Trumble, rising to her feet and dropping a curtsy. 'General Blackwood came to consult me about the amateur theatricals he means to hold at Mannerling for the amusement of the children. He acts the part of swain very well, as you witnessed.'

'Amateur theatricals!' Lady Beverley sat down and waved one thin white hand to indicate that Miss Trumble should serve tea. 'How amusing. Do you know, General, you are so convincing that for one mad moment I thought you were proposing marriage to Miss Trumble.' And Lady Beverley gave a silvery peal of laughter.

The general stood up abruptly. 'If you will excuse me, ladies, I do not think I will stay for tea after all. My son is returned from the search for Cater extremely exhausted, and I feel I should be with him.'

'As you will.' Lady Beverley looked somewhat huffy. She walked with him to his carriage, telling him that he really ought to have consulted her on the matter of theatricals—'for poor old Miss Trumble does not have our experience of the social scene, General.'

The general bowed without replying and entered the carriage and rapped on the roof for the coachman to drive on. He did not lower the glass to say any goodbyes. He had also forgotten to suggest to Miss Trumble that she might like to join the Blackwood household as governess.

'Such an odd creature,' murmured Lady Beverley to herself. 'But I shall have him yet!'

*   *   *

Rachel awoke very early the next morning and spent a long time choosing what to wear. At last she selected a muslin gown embroidered with little sprigs of lavender with deep flounces at the hem and little puffed sleeves. Then she went down to the parlour and sat by the window to wait.

The sun rose higher in the sky. She was joined about noon by Belinda and Lizzie, demanding to know if what Betty had told them was true—that the general had proposed to Miss Trumble.

Rachel turned reluctantly away from the window. 'Miss Trumble says he was merely rehearsing for some amateur theatricals, but I think she said that so as to save his face and not upset Mama.'

'But she could have been mistress of

Mannerling,' exclaimed Lizzie.

'There are still some sane people on this earth who do not want to be mistress of Mannerling,' said Rachel tartly. 'Do you not realize that every time one of us plots to regain Mannerling it all ends in shame and humiliation?'

'Meaning that now you know that Charles Blackwood will never propose to you,' said Belinda with a toss of her head, 'you pretend you never cared anyway.'

'And neither I do,' said Rachel. She turned wearily back to the window, her shoulders drooping.

'The children have not come this morning either,' said Lizzie.

Belinda joined Rachel at the window. 'Why, there is the carriage from Mannerling now. But it is only Mr. Charles, not the children. Oh, I hope the Blackwoods have not been offended by Miss Trumble and decided not to bring the children any more. I enjoyed their visits.'

They then heard Charles's voice in the hall, demanding to see Lady Beverley.

'There you are,' said Lizzie. 'He has come to complain about Miss Trumble.'

Rachel wanted to protest, to say that he had called to ask for her hand in marriage, but a superstitious fear kept her silent, as if long black shadows were reaching out over the fields from Mannerling to touch her very soul. Perhaps the house would have its revenge on her, and Charles would turn out to have called simply, as Lizzie had suggested, to complain about Miss Trumble.

She picked up a book and pretended to read. How the minutes dragged past.

And then the door swung open, to make her start and drop the book.

Lady Beverley sailed in.

'You are to go to the drawing-room, Rachel,' she said. 'Mr. Blackwood is desirous to pay his addresses to you. Oh, my dear child, you have succeeded where your sisters have failed. We will all soon be home again.'

But Rachel had already left.

She stood for a moment at the entrance to the drawing-room, looking shyly at Charles.

He silently opened his arms and she flew into them. He crushed her against him and kissed her passionately. Betty, the maid, outside the door, gave the couple a shocked look and quietly closed the door on the scene.

'Oh, my little love,' said Charles finally, 'you have not changed your mind?'

'No, but I feared you had when you did not call yesterday.'

'I was muddy and exhausted, in no state to propose marriage. My heart, I will keep Mannerling for you, if you wish.'

'Oh, no,' said Rachel with a shudder. 'I do not want the place. Just you, Charles.'

Which made him kiss her so passionately that when they finally surfaced, both of them were breathing raggedly.

He sat down and pulled her onto his knee. 'I must tell you now about my late wife. Had I not been so bitter about her flighty behaviour and so suspicious of every member of your sex, I swear I would have proposed to you that very first day, when I found you with my children at the lake.'

'You quite frightened me.'

'Am I too old for you?'

'No, beloved. Kiss me again.'

They finally broke apart when the door opened and Lady Beverley gave a loud cough. They stood together hand in hand as Lady Beverley came in, followed by Lizzie, Belinda, and Miss Trumble.

'Congratulate me,' said Charles. 'Rachel is to be my bride.'

Lizzie and Belinda gave cries of joy and ran to hug Rachel.

'And you will live at Mannerling,' cried Lizzie.

Rachel shook her head and smiled. 'Not Mannerling. We will live elsewhere.'

'Have you gone mad?' shrieked Lady Beverley.

Miss Trumble gave a little sigh and backed away and made her way through the back of the house and out into the garden.

She hailed Barry, who came over to join her. 'Such news, Barry,' said Miss Trumble. 'Rachel is to marry Charles Blackwood and they are so very much in love.' She sat down on a garden chair suddenly and, taking out a handkerchief, dabbed at her eyes.

Then she blew her nose firmly and went on, 'Dear me, I am quite overset. Such success! The fourth Beverley sister to marry well.'

'I did hear,' said Barry, looking down at her, his expression veiled, 'that the general proposed to you.'

'I have put it about that he was merely rehearsing a play, Barry, but yes, he did propose and I refused him.'

'Why, miss? You could have been set for life!'

'You mean, for what's left of it,' said the governess with a rueful grin. 'I am afraid I am one of those tedious romantics. I could not marry for anything other than love. Ridiculous at my age, is it not?'

Barry bent his grey head and pushed at the grass with the toe of one square-buckled shoe. 'Well, now, I do reckon that I am of the same mind, miss, or I'd ha' been spliced this long since.'

Miss Trumble rose. 'You are such a comfort to me, Barry. Now I must go and tell Betty to look in the cellar and see if we have any champagne left.'

She moved away across the grass and Barry stood for a moment looking after her before returning to his work.

CHAPTER SEVEN

*Whilst I have nobody but myself to
please, I have no one but myself to be
pleased with.*

Miss Weeton,
'Journal of a Governess 1807–1811.'

Minerva Santerton read the announcement of
Rachel's forthcoming wedding in the *Morning
Post* and threw the newspaper angrily across
the breakfast table at her brother.

'Rachel Beverley and Charles are to wed,'
she hissed.

He tossed the paper on the floor and looked
at her blearily. 'He told us that.'

'But I had begun to think it was all a hum,
that he only said it to get rid of us.'

'Even if that had been the case,' pointed out
George, 'then it stands to reason he didn't want
you.'

'Those brats of his turned him against me. I
hate children.'

'Just as well then that you ain't got any.'

The butler entered. 'There is a person called
to see you, Mrs. Santerton.'

'Miss,' said Minerva crossly.

'Don't know why you don't call yourself
"Mrs." Silly, I call it,' complained George,

'particularly when it looks as if you won't marry again and folks will forget you ever were married and think you're a spinster.'

Minerva ignored him and turned to the butler. 'We do not see persons,' she said. 'Tell whoever it is we are not at home.'

The door opened and Mr. Cater walked in.

He was travel-stained, his eyes were red with fatigue, and he strolled forward and sat down at the breakfast table.

Minerva nodded dismissal to the butler. 'What are you doing here?' she demanded. The scandal had not reached the newspapers in Sussex and she did not know Mr. Cater was being hunted down.

'I was in the neighbourhood,' said Mr. Cater, grabbing a fresh roll from a basket on the table and wolfing it. 'Remembered you had a place here.'

'I do not feel like guests at the moment,' said Minerva. 'You will find a good inn in the village.'

'This is no way to treat a fellow conspirator.' Mr. Cater rose and began to help himself to kidneys from the sideboard.

'Hey, what's all this about?' demanded George.

'I think you'd best leave Mr. Cater and me to have a private chat, George. Do run along.'

'All right, but send him on his way as soon as you can,' remarked George over his shoulder as he reached the door. 'He looks deuced odd.'

Mr. Cater, between gulps of food, told Minerva bluntly of how he had tried to have Miss Trumble harmed and then his rejection by Rachel and his subsequent flight.

Minerva listened, cold-eyed, until he had finished. Then she said, 'What I cannot understand is that if you wanted Mannerling, why did you not just make the Blackwoods an offer for it?'

'I thought if I wed one of those damned Beverley girls, the house would be securely mine. Judd, a previous owner, the one who killed himself, was my half-brother. He said had he married one of the Beverleys, the house would not have turned against him and his luck at the tables would have held.'

'Mad,' commented Minerva icily. 'Quite mad.'

'Anyway, I want to rack up here for a bit until the hunt dies down and then make my way to the coast.'

'I don't want you here.'

'If you don't put me up, sweeting, I'll write to Blackwood and tell him you were in the plot to get rid of that governess.'

She tightened her lips and her eyes flashed blue fire. 'You may stay a few days, that's all, and then go on your way.'

He looked down at his muddy clothes. 'I'll need some duds.'

'George has enough peacock finery for all the men in Bond Street. He will furnish you with something. After a few days, get you hence.'

Mr. Cater grinned. He had every intention of staying as long as possible.

*   *   *

To the further disappointment of Lady Beverley, Charles and Rachel refused to be married at Mannerling. Rachel and her family were to travel to London and stay with Abigail; Charles, the general, and the children would reside at their town house; and the pair would be married in London. Mannerling was already on the market for sale.

Belinda and Lizzie were to attend balls and parties during the Little Season, chaperoned by Abigail.

Miss Trumble believed she had fought another battle with Mannerling and won. As she helped with all the preparations for the journey, she felt the whole menace of Mannerling would soon be removed from their lives. All she had to do was to find husbands for Lizzie and Belinda.

She did not know that Belinda and Lizzie often wondered if anyone had made an offer for Mannerling. They were cross with Rachel because she refused to give them any information on the subject.

Rachel's reason for this was that Charles had told her that a certain Lord St. Clair had made a handsome offer. He was the son of the

Earl Durbridge, only twenty-four and not married. 'I shall keep that information from the girls and Mama,' Rachel told Charles. 'They will find out sooner or later, but I would rather it was later.'

But Lizzie and Belinda decided to call on Mary Judd, the vicar's daughter, one day shortly before they were due to go to London. Both detested Mary, but Mary was a good fund of gossip.

Mary gushed her usual welcome, but the smile on her lips never melted the hardness of her black eyes.

After various bits of chit-chat had been exchanged, Mary said, all mock sympathy, 'Such a pity Rachel is not to live at Mannerling. She must have been very disappointed.'

'On the contrary,' retorted Lizzie, 'Charles would have kept Mannerling if Rachel had wanted it, but Rachel wanted to live elsewhere.'

'Dear me! How odd! After all the Beverley ambitions.'

Belinda's beautiful eyes hardened. 'I trust you will not keep talking about the Beverley ambitions, Mary. That is in the past.'

Mary gave a little smile and poured tea. 'Then you will not be interested in the identity of the new owner.'

'A new owner already!' exclaimed Lizzie. 'Tell us. Who is it?'

'Oh, I am sure you are not interested.'

'Don't be infuriating, Mary,' said Belinda crossly. 'Who is buying Mannerling?'

'Perhaps it is a secret. I mean, apparently Rachel has said nothing to you ...'

'Do not trouble,' said Lizzie airily. 'Rachel will tell us. Do tell us instead the recipe for these cakes. Quite delicious.'

Mary gave her a baffled look and then said sulkily, 'It's a certain Lord St. Clair. Twenty-four and unwed. He is the eldest son of Earl Durbridge, and Mannerling is a present to his son. The earl is vastly rich and wishes to expand his property and possessions.'

To her disappointment, both Belinda and Lizzie affected indifference to this news and went on to beg for that recipe.

They had walked to the vicarage. When they left, Belinda and Lizzie sedately made their way along the country road under the turning leaves, but as soon as they were out of sight of the vicarage they stopped and clutched each other with excitement. All Lizzie's doubts and fears about Mannerling had left. Ambition had them in its grip again.

'It is your turn, Belinda,' said Lizzie fiercely. 'It is up to you.'

'Perhaps we can find out more about this lord in London,' said Belinda. 'We can ask Abigail. And we will be going to balls and parties and we can ask there. A rich young lord must be often talked about.'

213

'And let us keep this news to ourselves,' urged Lizzie, 'for if Miss Trumble thinks we have any interest in Mannerling, she might persuade Abigail or Rachel to keep us in London!'

* * *

Isabella and Rachel were walking in the grounds of Mannerling. 'I am so glad you and Fitzpatrick are to be here for my wedding,' said Rachel, 'and Mrs. Kennedy, too. I trust she is recovered from her fright.'

'She appears to be well,' said Isabella slowly, 'but do you know, she says she fears Mannerling. I tried to persuade her that the house only seemed haunted because of the machinations of that dreadful man, Cater.'

'There is no news of him.' Rachel looked uneasily around. 'I keep expecting him to return.'

'He would not dare! He has been exposed as a villain. Miss Trumble has found out more about him. As you know, he won those plantations of his at the gambling table, but the man he won them from was ruined as a result.'

'I am so glad none of us has the gambling fever,' said Rachel. 'Oh, there goes Mama, pursuing the general. I wish she would not. She is torturing the poor man. Mama hopes to secure him and persuade him not to sell. But Mannerling belongs to Charles. I have told her that many times, but she will not listen.'

'Did you tell her Lord St. Clair was to take the place?'

Rachel shook her head. 'I would not dare, nor Belinda or Lizzie either. They might not even go to London, anxious to stay rooted to the spot in case the new owner arrived when they were away.'

'Mama I can understand, but surely Belinda and Lizzie have grown out of that nonsense.'

'So they assure me and then they run off and whisper together, the way I used to run off and whisper to Abigail so that no one would guess our ambitions were still rampant.'

Isabella laughed. 'You should get a coat of arms and put on it two Beverleys rampant, with Mannerling in the middle. Here come your children. I will leave you to your play.'

Rachel ran to meet Mark and Beth. Isabella stood for a moment watching them and then walked slowly back to the house. If only Lizzie and Belinda could find happiness as well.

*   *   *

'Is that Cater fellow never going to leave?' grumbled George Santerton.

'You do something about it,' snapped Minerva, looking moodily out of the windows of the drawing-room at the dripping trees in the gardens. The autumn weather was chilly and wet and the good summer only a dim memory.

'By the way, the head gardener wants to get men in to lay a new path down to the pond.'

'Why?'

'That, sis, is where your late husband slipped, banged his head, and fell in the pond. Such unhappy memories.'

'Not unhappy. I am well rid of him. I never walk there and neither do you.'

'The present path, nonetheless, is slippery and precipitous.'

'And this, I may remind you, is my property and I am not going to any unnecessary expense.'

'As you will. Where's Cater now?'

'Out somewhere. How do we get rid of him? Think of something.'

'Shoot him?'

'Something sensible. The servants are already gossiping about our so-called Mr. Brown who arrived on a tired horse and with no luggage.'

Minerva suddenly swung round, her eyes shining. 'I have it. I will simply tell him that unless he goes, I will write to the authorities and tell them he is to be found here.'

'And they will wonder why we didn't tell them before.'

'We will say we did not know anything about it until now. But it is only a threat. But it will shift him.'

'You told me that he is wanted for an attack

on the governess and an assault on Rachel Beverley. You were not part of the plot by any chance, were you?'

'Don't be so stupid.' Minerva had suddenly realized that Mr. Cater had no proof that it was she who had suggested he put the governess out of action. Her blue eyes were shining with malice. 'I will go and find him and tell him now.'

'Do that, but take a gun with you.'

An undergardener weeding a flower-bed volunteered the information that 'Mr. Brown' had last been seen heading in the direction of the pond.

Minerva hesitated, but then set out towards where the pond lay. She walked across the wet lawns, the rings on her pattens making soggy imprints on the grass. She then entered the woods and walked on along a winding path where tall trees sent down showers of raindrops onto the calash she wore over her bonnet, until she could see ahead of her the gleam of water of the pond.

*   *   *

Ahead of her, Mr. Cater stood at the top of the precipitous muddy path which led down to the pond. So this was where the late Mr. Santerton had met his death. And no wonder. Why such a treacherous, steep, and muddy path should have been left on such an otherwise well-ordered estate puzzled Mr. Cater.

His mind worked busily. A couple more months here of free food and board and he would make his way to his bank in London before heading for the coast. He had not *killed* anyone. He shrewdly guessed that neither the Blackwoods nor the Beverleys would be anxious to keep the scandal alive.

What a dreary day! A thick mist was coiling around the boles of the dripping trees. And the days seemed long and tedious. He would try again that very evening, when George was in his cups, to get him to play a game of piquet. So far, George, even stupid with drink, had refused to gamble.

He shivered. What was he doing stumbling down this muddy path to view some dreary pond, not even an ornamental lake?

He half-turned to go back and his foot slipped. Cursing loudly, he slipped down and down the slippery path and plunged straight down into the icy waters of the pond.

He struggled and fought to rise, but thick weeds at the bottom were wrapped round his ankles. He finally tore free and with bursting lungs his head broke the surface.

'Help!' he shouted. 'I can't swim.'

Minerva stopped just above the pond and heard that shout. She turned very white and began to tremble. The mist was so eerie, she was sure she was hearing the voice of her dead husband. Had she not stood just here and heard him cry for help. As if in a nightmare, she turned as she had turned then and began to hurry away, back up the hill and through the trees, the cries growing fainter behind her as they had done on that dreadful day when her drowning husband's struggles had made him hit his head on a rock before he sank for the last time. That had been the coroner's deduction at the inquest.

It was only when she had stumbled into the hall of her home that her wits cleared and she remembered that she had gone to find Mr. Cater.

George came down the stairs and stopped short at the sight of his sister.

'You look as if you have seen a ghost,' he said.

'Quickly,' hissed Minerva, 'into the library.'

He followed her in and stood looking inquiringly at her. The little-used room was musty and lined with books which had not been taken down and read since the last century.

'What is it?' demanded George. 'Is it Cater? Did he attack you?'

She shook her head.

'Then what is it?'

'I went down to the pond to find Cater,' said Minerva in a dull voice. 'A gardener said he had gone that way. I was approaching the pond and I heard a cry for help, and someone shouting, "I can't swim." I turned and walked away.'

'I'd best get the men and get down there. It was Cater. He was saying the other night that he had never learned to swim.'

'Wait! It will be too late now. He will be dead, and we will need to report that death if the servants know about it. And it will come out that we have been harbouring Cater.'

'And if it does? We will say we knew nothing of the trouble at Mannerling.'

'Who would believe us? The servants will say he arrived in a state and without luggage and has been going by the name of Brown.'

George looked at her uneasily. 'You were implicated some way in those goings-on at Mannerling. You must have been or you would not have allowed him to stay. And that's what happened to poor Santerton. It was an accident but you could have saved him, but you walked away.'

'Stop going on about what I am supposed to have done. The problem is that we must get Cater's body, which is no doubt floating on the pond, and bury it. According to the servants, he has gone off and that is that.'

'I tell you, sis, I will help you, but then I will take myself off. It's like living with Lady Macbeth.'

'You always were a weakling, George!'

'Oh, God, spare me your insults. Let us see if we can still save the poor man.'

'The servants must not see us!'

'We'll just go for a little walk. It's dark now. I will take a lantern.'

Soon they set out together, George holding the lantern high as they finally negotiated the slippery path.

They stood on a grassy knoll at the side of the treacherous path. George swung the lantern in a wide arc.

'Nothing,' he whispered. 'He's probably up in my room, looking dry clothes out of my wardrobe.'

'Wait!' urged Minerva, 'Try near the edge.'

George held the lantern out over the bottom of the path and Minerva drew back against him with a little hiss.

The body of Mr. Cater lay almost directly below them, his hands stretched out grasping the mud. He had obviously managed to nearly get out of the water, but cold and exhaustion had robbed him of his final strength.

'It's going to be a day's work to drag him up that path and bury him,' muttered George. 'I say we put some rocks in his pockets and push him back in the pond.'

'You do it,' shivered Minerva. 'I could not bear to touch him.'

George gave her a look of loathing. 'I'll do it during the night. Let's go back.'

At two o'clock that morning, George, with a bag of rocks and some heavy chains over his shoulder, made his way back to the pond. He worked quickly, weighing down the pockets of

221

Mr. Cater's body with rocks, and then wrapping the chain around his legs. He then gave the body a huge push and heard a sinister gurgling sound as it sank beneath the waters of the pond.

And then he went wearily back to the house to get well and truly drunk.

*   *   *

Mrs. Kennedy walked about the grounds of Mannerling the following day. There was a steel-cold wind from the east. She and Isabella and Lord Fitzpatrick were to leave for London on the following day. She had been drawn to visit Mannerling one last time, to walk the lawns and say a prayer for the dead footman. She thought she would never forget John's scream as he fell from the roof.

She went to sit in the folly and look out over the black waters of the lake. The folly was the only place at Mannerling that she really liked, possibly because it had been built on the orders of Charles Blackwood and was not part of the old Mannerling.

She had kept her doubts about the two remaining Beverley sisters, Belinda and Lizzie, to herself, not wanting to worry Isabella. She sensed that neither Belinda nor Lizzie had given up their ambitions to reclaim their old home. What a passion the wretched place aroused in people! Only think of that creature,

222

Cater.

She left the folly and walked down to the lake. The wind abruptly died and the waters were cold and still.

'It's goodbye to you, Mannerling,' said Mrs. Kennedy. 'If I have my way, neither I nor Isabella will ever come here again.'

Then she suddenly felt colder than the day itself and a mist seemed to surround her. She was standing on the jetty and a white face grinned up at her from the water. She let out a hoarse scream and crossed herself.

As if waking from a nightmare, she looked around and found there was no mist at all. She looked back down at the lake again. There was no face in the water.

She turned and began to hurry back towards where her carriage was parked outside the house. She never told anyone about her experience or that the face in the water that she thought she had seen had looked like the dead face of Mr. Cater.

*　　　*　　　*

Rachel and Charles were married on a winter's day in London in St. George's, Hanover Square. Lady Beverley wept noisily throughout the service. After all, sensibility was all the rage.

Miss Trumble felt quietly satisfied. Another happy ending. She sat at the back of the church, heavily veiled. In fact, her veil was so heavy that Barry, also at the back of the church, remarked slyly that it was almost as if she did not want any of the fashionables among the guests to recognize her.

Belinda, as bridesmaid, wondered if she herself could ever look forward to such happiness. The church was cold and she shivered in her fur-lined cloak. She and Lizzie had attended a few balls and routs and also the playhouse, but nowhere had they seen the mysterious Lord St. Clair. They heard of him, however, heard he was in London, and that he was regarded as one of the most eligible men on the marriage market. They also learned that he preferred town life and that his father had bought him Mannerling in the hope that a house and lands of his own would give him more responsibility and encourage him to take a bride.

Abigail had offered them a Season in London, and both Lizzie and Belinda had decided to accept. If their quarry preferred town life, then surely he would emerge at the following Season.

Beside Belinda, Lizzie was feeling uncomfortable, for Mrs. Kennedy had given her a stern talking-to only the day before. Lizzie was very fond of Mrs. Kennedy but had not liked being told that Mannerling was a wicked place. She quite forgot that she had thought that very thing herself not so long ago.

That old ambition was burning in her veins. Belinda must somehow manage to marry Lord St. Clair. Lizzie went off into a dream of sunny days at Mannerling, back home again, and only came out of it as she realized her sister, Rachel, was well and truly married and the bells were ringing out in triumph over the sooty buildings of London.

The wedding breakfast was held in the Blackwoods' town house, which had once been the Beverley town house. It was to be sold as well. The Blackwoods would not be returning to Mannerling again. They had cleared out all their possessions from the place. The town house did not have too many memories for the Beverley sisters, for they had spent most of their time at Mannerling. Only Isabella had made her come-out from the town house, remembering, as she sat next to her husband, what a disaster that had been. She had been so haughty and proud, she had thought no man good enough for her.

A small orchestra was playing sweet melodies. The room was full of the happy sound of conversation.

Rachel sat at the top table beside her new husband, happy and content. Charles was buying a property outside Deal on the coast. Until they were ready to move in, they would travel here and there on their honeymoon and end up in Ireland to stay with Isabella. The Fitzpatricks were returning there after the wedding.

She floated on a happy dream through the breakfast and the dancing afterwards, until it was time to leave.

Her sisters clustered on the pavement outside the town house to wave goodbye. She felt a lump in her throat as she kissed them one after the other, then her mother and then Miss Trumble.

Rose-petals were thrown, handkerchiefs waved. Rachel leaned out of the carriage window and waved back until the carriage turned the corner and her past life was lost to view. She put up the glass, blew her nose firmly, and said huskily, 'I can only pray that Belinda and Lizzie will be as happy as I am.'

'As to that, I hope they will,' said Charles, 'although, if you remember, we attended Mrs. Dunster's party a few weeks ago. I did not tell you then, for I did not want to distress you, but I fear both Lizzie and Belinda were overheard asking curious questions about Lord St. Clair.'

Rachel looked alarmed. 'They must know! We must turn back. I must talk to them, warn them.'

'No, my sweeting, the estimable Miss Trumble has been warned by me and will do all in her power to keep them safe.'

He put an arm around her and held her close. 'Kiss me, Mrs. Blackwood. And if you ever mention Mannerling again, I shall beat you.'

'Would you, indeed!'

'Probably not. Kiss me instead.'

Rachel did as she was bid, and after a long while she said dreamily, 'I hope Mark and Beth will not miss us too much.'

'They are so excited to be going to Ireland with your sister, they have probably forgotten about us already.'

'When does St. Clair take up residence?'

'I really should beat you. Five kisses for that. I do not know. It is his father who wants him to remove to the country and away from the wickedness of Town. I think it will be a long time before he goes there. Now for those kisses...'

*　　　*　　　*

Lord St. Clair at that moment was facing his father. He was a tall, willowy young man dressed in the latest Bond Street fashion, which made him look like an elegant wasp. His waist was pinched in with a corset and his vest was of black and gold stripes. 'Don't think I want that Mannerling place after all,' he drawled.

'What?' demanded the choleric earl. 'Most beautiful place in the world, and you turn your nose up at it.'

'My agent went to look at it,' said Lord St. Clair with weary sigh. 'Man, very reliable, my agent. Stout fellow. Says the place is haunted.'

'Pah! Fustian. Been at the brandy, that's

227

what he's been doing. Get rid of him.'

'He went down to sort out the servants, you know, which to keep and which to send packing, and a lot of 'em told him the place was haunted by some chap who hanged himself from the chandelier and, worse than that...'

'Oh, do tell, you popinjay! A headless horseman?'

'No, a drowned man.'

The earl took a deep breath. 'Now listen to me, m'boy, you are not going to spend your life racketing around London. You can get yourself a suitable gel at the next Season, move to Mannerling and set up your nursery, or I will disinherit you!'

Lord St. Clair took out a scented handkerchief and waved it in front of his painted face, as if perfume could sweeten his father's temper.

'You wouldn't do that,' he protested.

'Oh, yes, I would. It's Mannerling, a bride, or nothing.'

St. Clair uncoiled himself from his chair and headed for the door. 'As you will, Father,' he said in a mournful voice. 'As you will.'

He strolled round to Bond Street to comfort himself and fell in with two equally elegant cronies.

'You look like the deuce,' said one. 'What's amiss?'

'Got the threat of the country hanging over me,' mourned St. Clair. 'Father says he'll disinherit me if I don't get meself a bride at the next Season and move to that place Mannerling he's bought me.'

'Do as he says,' counselled the other. 'Move to Mannerling and take the Town down with you, big parties, good friends, good bottles, and a complacent wife, and as soon as she's produced the heir, take yourself back to Town.'

'Jove, the very idea,' said St. Clair, brightening. 'The countryside will never have seen anything like us. Mannerling it is!'

The LARGE PRINT HOME LIBRARY

If you have enjoyed this Large Print book and would like to build up your own collection of Large Print books and have them delivered direct to your door, please contact The Large Print Home Library.

The Large Print Home Library offers you a full service:

☆ **Created to support your local library**

☆ **Delivery direct to your door**

☆ **Easy-to-read type & attractively bound**

☆ **The very best authors**

☆ **Special low prices**

For further details either call Customer Services on 01225 443400 or write to us at:

The Large Print Home Library
FREEPOST (BA 1686/1)
Bath BA2 3SZ